# BLACK
*is for*
# HATE

BLACK IS FOR HATE

Want to know about Michael's new books?
Sign up for his new release newsletter at:
kowalkowal.com

Telling
Stories
Press

# Other Books By Michael Kowal

<u>John Devin, PI — The Novels</u>
  Red is for Blood (Book 1)
  Black is for Hate (Book 2)
  Gold is for Greed (Book 3) — coming soon…

<u>John Devin, PI — Short Stories</u>
  Sunshine (No. 1)
  Bennie (No. 2)

# YOUR FREE STORY IS WAITING

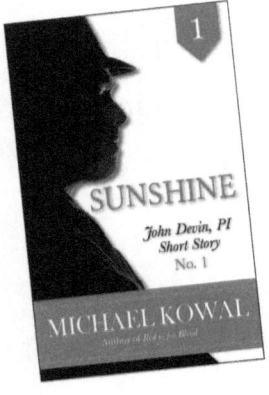

It's 1930s Los Angeles and ex-Marine, and current PI, John Devin tackles his first case...

...get back millions of dollars stolen from Little Jackie Sunshine — America's famous child star.

The problem? Her rancid mother is the one who stole it. All of it.

For Devin there's only one way to go — get it back.
Any way possible.

*"If you like your PIs hard boiled and with attitude, get Sunshine — a perfect storm where old Hollywood, an ex-Marine PI, and a very bad mother — meet."*

Your free story - Sunshine - is waiting for you at:

kowalkowal.com/free-story

Get It Now!

# Acknowledgments

First and foremost, I would like to thank my wife. Without her support, love, and incredibly calming good sense, I would never be able to do this. Any of it. To her I give my greatest thanks, and forever, all of my love.

To my amazing first readers — Tracy, Lee Ann, Mike and Tom — you turned it around fast, then helped me see what I couldn't see, and catch what I couldn't catch. This book couldn't have been what it is without you. Thank you.

To Allyson Longueira, who's input helped shape the covers and branding for the entire John Devin series, many thanks. Thanks also to Colleen Kuehne my master copy editor who amazes me with everything she finds, corrects, and helps me make better.

A great big thanks to Bob@LAPoliceMuseum for taking the time to answer some basic questions, to help make things a little more accurate. And as usual, the USC Digital Library was an invaluable resource with photos and other research material that helped me ground the story in 1930s LA.

And finally to Kristine Kathryn Rusch, Dean Wesley Smith, ML Buchman, everyone at Sunday Lunch, and everyone in the Oregon Writer's Network — you've all offered such incredible advice, support, inspiration, and help, I don't know that I'll ever be able to repay all of you but please, accept this thanks as a token of the love and appreciation I have for each of you.

*To Tracy*

*my first, and best, true fan…*

# Chapter 1

CARLO LOVED THE BASEMENT.

Ben Bernie's "Crazy Rhythm," a fox-trot, poured out of the gramophone along the wall. A nice little ditty, complete with *smack, smacks* that sounded, honest to God, like someone actually smacking somebody. Carlo had to laugh at that one.

Then, inside the basement, another punch hit home with the muffled sound of fist to thigh.

Yes, Carlo's black-and-blue party.

The music and the hitting in the basement kept going as Carlo remembered the fight of the century — the Tunney-Dempsey fight — three years back in 1927. In Chicago.

Carlo was there, and even through the sound of the crowd you could hear Tunney land the punches on Dempsey. *Smack, smack*. The fight went all the way for a decision but Carlo knew all along that Tunney had it. His fists were steel, and they landed like hammers.

Another punch smacked in the basement, this time with a dull thud to a shoulder, Baldy doing all of the hitting.

Patty lay on the bed, tied up, naked except for the clean rag in her mouth. She wanted that, because she knew how much Carlo hated the screaming.

Baldy stood there on the other side of the bed from Patty. He looked like an undertaker in his white shirt and black pants. He was tall, way too tall, and his head almost scraped the open boards of the ceiling above. He was funny looking, Carlo thought. Sweat shined from his bald dome, little bits of his black hair, whatever he had of it, plastering themselves on top of his head.

Baldy looked happier than a pig in shit.

But inside, Carlo knew he was mean. Maybe he was so mean — because he was bald.

Carlo would never call him Baldy to his face, at least not yet, but that was about to change. Things always changed when you put the bite on people.

Baldy cocked his arm for another smack, then drove his fist down into Patty. At least he kept to the thighs and shoulders, like they agreed. Not like that first time when he went a little crazy and went — a little too far.

That wasn't so good. But in the end, it wasn't so bad either.

Like Carlo always said — if the world gives you lemons, you make money off of it.

And with what Baldy did, and the couple more times he did it, Carlo was going to make him pay — a lot.

See, Baldy was a lawyer, and he had a lot of money. He lived in the hills above Beverly Hills, up a road near the top. Maybe Carlo would pay him a little visit there soon. Have some fun with him. Tell him how much it was going to cost to keep Carlo quiet.

Baldy stepped back away from the bed and rolled his shoulder. He'd been at it for a while now, the poor guy. Then he smiled at Carlo.

Carlo smiled right back at him. He hated the son of a bitch.

"Crazy Rhythm" was almost over. Couldn't let that happen, so Carlo walked over to the gramophone. He had to keep the music going so Baldy didn't hear anything come from the other room. He wouldn't like what was going on over there. Not one little bit.

Carlo pulled out another record, a John Philip Sousa march — it had a nice beat.

Carlo laughed.

That was rich.

The record started, Carlo turned up the sound, and Baldy just kept on hitting.

It all sounded like money to Carlo.

Money on the way to the bank.

# Chapter 2

I REALLY HATE TUESDAYS.

It's report day.

And that's exactly why I was sitting in front of my Washington 5C safe. Six feet tall of black steel, doubled-doored, double-handled, and with a reputation of being uncrackable. And I'd already done it three times. But of course, the last time was eight months ago. So I was out of practice.

It was only eleven in the morning and already I'd wasted two hours on the Washington. But I liked doing it. It was calming for me. Like women knitted, I cracked safes. It's why I had seven of them in my office.

I had my frosted glass door closed so Bella, outside, couldn't see what I was doing. Or not doing. As in the reports.

She was my secretary and I guess you could say served the purpose of a master sergeant, kicking my backside whenever she felt like I wasn't getting done what needed to be done. Even though I owned the joint. I supposed that's why I liked her.

She put up with me.

The joint was John Devin Investigations and I was the PI of the outfit. An ex-Marine landed in LA after serving in Europe for the great tea party the world threw for us there, plus a bit of time in China playing tag with revolutionaries, the only thing I was good at was handling a gun and fighting.

So of course I became a PI. What the hell else was I going to do, be a movie star?

I stepped back away from the Washington and cracked my neck twice just to get the kinks out, then walked over to one of the windows on 7th to see if the world was still there.

It was. From the second story of a two-story building, the view wasn't bad.

My office was in the corner of the building at 7th and Carol. I had one window on Carol and two on 7th, but 7th always had the action. It was a major street that headed out of downtown Los Angeles, and ran west toward the Pacific Ocean a ways away.

The sidewalk below me was filled with men in hats, women in hats, and everybody heading wherever it was they were heading. Unfortunately it wasn't into my office. But nobody had any money these days for cases. The stock market crash took care of all that.

A brand new, long-as-a-battleship, apple red Duesenberg came down 7th, its polished chromium grille flaring back the LA sun like a mirror. The engine ran whisper quiet as it drove past, like the great thing was gliding along on a slab of air. Somebody with a lot more money than me.

Two raps hit at my door. I hoped it wasn't Bella. "Come in."

It was Bella.

Bella was a broad and a half. She was bigger than most women, with all the curves in all the right places. Big boned, I guess you could say, with mahogany hair pulled back in loose waves away from her face, and always with the red lips.

Her eyes were as brown as her hair, her makeup always perfect, and I fought with her like an older sister I never had. Well, maybe ends up, I did have one.

The only problem with Bella today was she wore her bright yellow blouse with the floppy collar.

Which meant she had on her black skirt. The one with the

buttons up the right side, and that — meant trouble. Whenever she wore that skirt and that blouse, I knew she was in a bad mood. "Keeping yourself busy?"

I got behind my desk. "Yeah, doing the reports as ordered."

"Bull." She looked over at the Washington. "Get it open yet?" She always knew.

"No."

"Don't worry, Junior. Some day."

"Is that all you came in for?"

"Yeah." She smiled, all sly. "And, you got someone here to see you."

"Well, why don't you get your beautiful self out of the way so they can come in."

"Always sweet-talking me."

I nodded toward my twin-rig shoulder holsters hanging from the coat rack behind me, filled with two great big guns. "I can use those things."

"In your dreams."

Then she got herself out of the door and let someone else come in.

Rose.

Rose never came to the office.

Ever.

# Chapter 3

ROSE WAS A MADAM. And not the kind that you met at a tea party.

She walked in, in her usual long, flowing red dress trimmed in lace like something straight out of a… well, a whorehouse.

She was a solid woman, walked like a rock with legs, and had rust-colored hair that frizzed down her head like dirty sea foam. She was probably something in her day, but now her face was on the puffy side, with a small nose and a large mouth with deep red lipstick the color of her dress.

She was always tired, her face looked like it never saw the light of day, and all in all she was who she was. And she was all right in my book.

"Rose." I came out from behind my desk and helped her to one of the two red leather chairs in front of my desk. "How are you?"

"If I said good, would you believe me?" Her voice was raspy and breathless, like cigarette smoke.

"Not a bit."

"Neither would I." She shifted in her seat and looked at all seven safes scattered against the walls. "You a collector or something?" The way she said it was like she was asking after an uncle who had gone crazy.

"A little. I like to play with them."

She looked back at me. "Good for you." I don't think she believed it.

Rose had been around for a while and I'd used her a few times when I needed information. Usually we met downtown at the Angel Diner on Hill. Have breakfast, do a little talking. Her, coming here, it was definitely different. "So Rose, what can I do for you?"

"I got a girl…"

She had a lot of girls. She ran the Pacific Surf Hotel for the System.

The System was the crime syndicate that ran everything fun that happened in LA — booze, gambling, and women. All of it.

Where Chicago had Capone, LA had the System. A kinder and more genteel way of doing business. No shootings, no killings, and no psychotic lunatic running things. Well, one out of three wasn't bad.

Rose looked out the window onto 7th a bit, I suppose to get her thoughts together. "Her name is Holly."

I grabbed the small pad and red pencil from my desk and wrote down the name. Cases usually started with one. I underlined it. It made it real. "Holly."

"Holly Scanveld. She came in through another one of the girls three years ago. They met at the automat on Third." Rose stopped.

I'd never seen her so quiet. Usually we'd get our business done and that was that, but there was something here that was different.

Rose took a breath, sat up straight, and her face went strong. "Holly came in, ready to work, and that was that."

"How old is she?"

"Twenty-five." Rose reached into a pocket of her dress. "I forgot," she said, and pulled out a small photo and handed it to me. "Holly."

It was taken in a more formal setting. It was black and white and shades of gray, a girl of eighteen maybe, sitting on a padded chair and looking prim. Holly.

She was young in the photo, blond hair streaming down in long waves. Her mouth was small and had an almost smile, her eyes looked playful — like she was having the time of her life getting her photograph taken.

"She gave it to me." Rose took a deep breath, digging for strength.

I looked back up to Rose, "She from LA?"

"From Montana. A spunky little thing." Rose smiled when she said it. "Not much bigger than a kid, seemed to me, but she was strong. Got tired of the cold, and her parents."

I could relate. At least the old man part of it.

"Father was a second-rate preacher, mother the doorstop. Holly came out to Los Angeles for a little fun. And the sun."

"Actress?"

"Dancer. She made it into a couple of pictures. But that was pretty much that."

"So what's going on with her now?"

"I haven't heard from her."

"How long?"

"Three days."

That was all? I'd been on benders longer than three days. "She's twenty-five, Rose."

But there was something else on my mind, and I didn't like it.

Lately, there were some really bad things happening to women in LA. Really bad.

To women like Holly.

"It's… just a feeling."

Okay. I've learned to trust feelings; they're all right in my book. Saved me more than once, and solved more than enough cases for me. It was like a little voice in the back of my head, and I listened to it. "What's your feeling?"

Rose looked down at her lap. She took a couple deep breaths that rattled just the slightest in her chest, like something was coming for her. "Before she disappeared, she called and said she wouldn't be in. She said she had family in town."

"What's wrong with that?"

Rose looked up at me. "She didn't have any family."

"What do you mean? You said she had a mother and father. That's family in my book."

Rose smirked, and not a nice one. "The mother would never leave the father, and the father would never come here."

It was the way she said it. "Why?"

Then Rose's smirk became a downright sneer. "Because the last time Holly saw him, she nearly cut off his thing."

"As in…" I raised my eyebrow.

Rose's answer was a flat, "Yeah."

I wasn't sure where this was heading, and I didn't much want to hear any more. I had a bad feeling now, too. "He try something with her?"

"Yeah." There was nothing else.

Some days you don't like what you hear in life. You wish you could un-hear it. Wish it never happened. You wish you could kill a guy who would do something like that to his own daughter. "How old was she?"

"Sixteen."

And that was that. I got the picture. "Is she seeing anyone? Outside of work?" I wasn't sure that a prostitute would. My guess was you wouldn't want to see a guy again after… everything she did in a day.

"No. There was a guy a year ago maybe that was hanging around. She seemed to like him a lot. I thought they'd settle down."

"What happened?"

"He just up and left." Rose didn't seem too happy about it. "Broke her up real bad. She actually stopped working for a while."

"You think he came back?"

Rose took in a labored breath. "No. She would have told me."

I wasn't so sure. "She tell you everything?"

Rose looked at me like she was about to hit me. "Look, Devin, I don't get close to a lot of my girls, but… there was something about Holly."

"What?"

As the sun came in from the windows over 7th, it shone in Rose's eyes and I could see them glisten... almost wet enough to fall. But she didn't let anything fall. She was tough. "All right, she reminded me of myself, all right? Not like I felt sorry for her or anything, not at all. That girl could—" and Rose stopped herself short. She took a deep breath as if to push something down and her eyes now looked like they were really going to let loose. "She's a strong one, that one. The strongest. The way she handled her old man," Rose smiled, "I couldn't think of nothing better." Then the smile faded. "Find her, Devin, all right?"

"I will, Rose." But I wasn't so sure. The little feeling in the back of my head didn't like this. Not one bit.

Rose gave me a few other things on Holly, just basics like her home address, and let me keep the photo. Then she got up out of the chair and got herself to the door to the outer office. "I know there's been things happening to girls lately."

She knew, too.

"To girls like her."

To prostitutes. Exactly like Holly, and that, I tried to push out of my head.

"Just find her, Devin. She deserves it."

Then Rose was out my door and out the outer office door like a shot. Probably to beat the waterworks.

I stood there in my office, hoping Holly was gone for some good reason. Like the nice guy came back to marry her. Or she decided to get a different job. Anything.

But that place at the back of my head wouldn't let me stop thinking that, maybe, she didn't do any of those things. Maybe... it was worse.

# Chapter 4

ROSE WAS ONLY GONE a second, and already the voices started up in the outer office.

"I ain't," said Charlie.

I walked out to see what was going on.

Charlie was only fifteen, but was already a shade shorter than six foot. Which meant just a shade-and-a-half shorter than me. He was finally getting back a little of the baby fat after getting some food in him. I hired him after his old man kicked him out of the house — right during this *depression*, as Hoover called it.

I couldn't even think of it.

Charlie was big, sturdy, and more than a little sharp, if not a little dazed at being a kid forced to join a grownup world ahead of his time. He did odd jobs around the office, anything to keep him busy. And Bella, was the one to keep him busy.

"I ain't doing any more of it." Charlie was a good kid, running into a steamroller.

"Don't use *ain't*. It's not a word."

These two were why I shut my door to begin with. Two hours ago. "What's going on?"

Bella's small area, the outer office and the official reception area of John Devin Investigations, was a small ten by fifteen, with exactly one desk — hers — two chairs against the wall — the clients' — and a stand ashtray between the chairs, a lamp in the corner, and a small table under the one window that looked out onto 7th.

Bella sat at her desk, and Charlie stood against the far wall — and I was not getting between them.

Bella smiled at Charlie and nodded toward me. "Go ahead, tell him." She said it like a hangman, getting ready a noose.

"Well, Mr. Devin…" He swallowed. "I've been filing things for the past five weeks it seems like."

Bella snorted. "You haven't even been here four."

Charlie looked at her, and I watched as he got a little bit of his backbone up. Then he looked at me. "For however long — and I want to help with something else. Please."

I felt sorry for the kid. I'd seen the razor-thin lines of red that cut across his fingers. Paper cuts. I hated the damn things. I'd been shot, knifed, cut, beat up, and woke hungover from a five-day drinking binge in a back alley in Singapore, and nothing — I mean *nothing* — more I hated than paper cuts. "Sorry, kid." And I was. "I can't help you. Bella needs you to file things, then that's what you gotta do." I was smart that way — stay out of her way.

I hired Charlie in the spur-of-the-moment the day he walked in looking for work. Because his old man had thrown him out of the house. I needed him like I needed a hole in the head. So I hired him anyway.

One of my momentary moments of weakness.

But I had no idea what to do with the kid. He was fifteen. And what could fifteen do? Of course, I had already done a lot by the age of sixteen. War did that for you. But I was glad he didn't have to do anything like I had to. At least he wouldn't have to if I could help it. But even though the kid was looking at me like a drowning guy looking for a life preserver, there was no way I was going to get in the middle of him — and Bella. "Just listen to her, kid."

And I got the hell out of there.

I'd learned a long time ago to pick my battles, and Bella was not one of them. But now, Holly was.

And I was going to find her.

I hoped I was going to find her.

And I prayed that she was going to be alive.

# Chapter 5

PEOPLE MISSING EITHER WANTED to be, or they didn't want to be, and that was the question.

No disrespect meant to Mr. Shakespeare.

So either Holly went off for some reason on her own, or something had happened. It's usually my experience that when someone goes "missing," they want to be. And after only three days missing, there were any number of reasons she could be gone.

Skipping town because of a debt, or to get away from the cops, or just to get a little restlessness out of their system. You know, you hear a radio program about Florida and you think, why not?

On the other side of the ledger, that's where most people's minds go. The Roses of the world. They think they're either dead, kidnapped, or lying in a gutter somewhere. I guess I get it. You're scared for them. Or rather, you're scared for what you'd have to deal with if things really did go bad.

We don't want to face that. Nobody does. Nobody in their right mind does, but if there's one thing I've learned doing what I do, it's that there are a good lot of people out there who aren't in their right mind. At least not a right mind that any of us would agree to.

So I got to Holly's apartment, fast.

She lived on Alexandria just north of 4th, only a few blocks from the Hollywood Royal Hotel. A nice area, actually. Not expensive, but not cheap.

Mostly made up of huge brick apartment buildings, Holly lived in the only courtyard bungalow building on the block. Not a building, actually, but seven individual white… homes. They looked like their own simple versions of houses, but all gathered together in a U shape with a small sidewalk running up the middle, and about five square feet of grass out front of each of them. They weren't fancy, but they were nice judging from the road. Well kept.

Which meant neighbors that cared. Not exactly a place you wanted to be breaking into through the front door, especially since the front doors all faced each other.

I kept driving and parked in front of the big brick building up the road.

There weren't a lot of brick buildings in Los Angeles, what with the earthquakes and all, but when you found them, they had usually been standing for a while.

They either drop, or stay. There isn't much in between.

I had a number for Holly's bungalow, four, but I needed to find out just where that was. So I walked casually past the apartments and spotted a two on the one facing me as I walked past, did a quick turn to see the one on the one I'd just passed. Odds to the left, evens to the right.

I was looking for the middle unit on the right side facing in. Easy.

I kept walking until I got two more buildings down, then ducked between the two larger brick buildings and made my way to the alley in back.

I liked alleys. Respectable people kept out of them, and any people in them, they tended to keep to themselves and not bother anyone else. The only problem was lately there were a lot more people in them.

Ever since the crash, I'd noticed a lot more people on the

street. You lose your job, you do what you can to keep yourself fed and a roof over your head. And your family, too.

It's like a giant rug got shaken, and what was going on now was the settling of all the dust.

There were more people out on the street, and a lot more back in the alleys. Everyone, I guess, trying to figure out where it was they were supposed to settle now.

You did what you could to feed yourself. And anyone else that depended on you.

I got to the back of the apartments and there was a fresh wood fence put up. I suppose to keep out the riffraff.

I didn't consider myself riffraff, so I figured I was just welcome to go on in.

I lifted the small, black iron latch on the outside and pushed my way in through the plain wooden door. Inside, I faced the back of a bungalow. The bungalow at the bottom of the U from what I could see.

The bungalow was raised up on a small foundation, with a single window in back that faced toward me from a few feet up. I stepped a bit to my left to get out of its way.

The window itself had nice white curtains draped on either side, with a red geranium blooming in a small pot sitting on the windowsill. A woman's place.

The back area of the place was simple packed dirt, with two garbage cans, older than the fence, tucked in the left corner.

I walked around those and into the very small walkway up the back of the bungalows on that side. The path to Holly's place.

I passed soft and fast behind one bungalow and got to the middle one, Holly's.

There was no geranium in the window that I could tell, because the window shade was pulled tight against everything from the outside.

Two small, bare wood steps led up to the white back door, so I walked up to them, put on a pair of thin leather gloves, and pulled out my set of lock picks. Handy things to have when you're out for a stroll.

Ended up I didn't need them, the door was unlocked. That I didn't like. So I put away my picks and pulled out my guns.

Now I don't usually need them, but I like to carry them: twin Colt 1911 .45s with ivory handles. I carry them mostly because they tend to calm people down on the other end of me pointing them. Or if not calm them down, calm down their ideas of doing anything to me that I don't want done.

Holly, I figure, is smart. Most working girls are, and judging by the way she handled her old man, she can take care of herself. And the first step in doing that is keeping your doors locked. Hers wasn't. And I wasn't sure what that meant.

I opened the door with my free hand and listened.

Nothing.

The air inside the place smelled closed, like it hadn't been disturbed for a while.

Like maybe for three days.

Okay, so maybe Rose was a little on the right side. I got myself inside and shut the door.

It was the kitchen, and it was small. Maybe only six feet wide, with a white porcelain sink and a small counter to the left, and some white cabinets to the right. Then I noticed water on the floor.

To my right, behind the door and below the back window, was a white metal icebox about three feet tall and two feet across. It had one tall door on the left, and two smaller doors on the right, stacked one above the other, and all the doors with black hinges and handles. It was small as iceboxes go but it did the trick, especially if there was only one person using it.

Below the icebox was the drain pan and that pan was full to overflowing.

Someone hadn't emptied it and my guess was it had probably been about… three days. It wasn't scientific, just putting things together.

The place was quiet as a tomb, but I held one .45 out in front of me just in case.

I didn't need it. A quick walk out into the rest of the small place let me know there was no one there.

A small living room sat in front of the kitchen, with a single window facing out to the rest of the courtyard. The shade was down on that window, too, and a little bit of sunlight speared in through the two sides.

The living room itself was simple. Two oak chairs sat against the wall that was shared with the kitchen, the shaded window that faced outside was opposite it, and in the corner next to the window sat a small dark table with a small radio on top of it. A clean white tablecloth with lace sat under the radio, and for some reason it looked out of place. I didn't know why, but it did. The rest of the place was simple and no frills, but the tablecloth got me.

I walked over to it and a single framed photo sat on the table next to the radio.

The frame was dark and thin but looked to be of sturdy wood. The photo itself was of a woman in her early forties, maybe. The land was open around her with what looked to be the edge of a barn or some large wooden building to the right. The land was flat and the dirt tilled. A farm, definitely. I knew farms.

The woman had a rough face from being out in the elements, but also in it was the peace of someone who worked the land. Almost peace. But looking at the edges of her face, you could feel something else, like she had been plowed up like the field that lay exposed around her. My guess was, Holly's mother.

I could see the appeal of Los Angeles to a girl raised on a farm like that. In a home like that. The photo was the only piece of personal anything in the place.

I took a quick look in the bedroom: a small iron bed with no frills and a side table to match, only in brown-painted wood. Dinged and marred.

Everything was put away, nothing left out, and nothing to tell me who Holly was, besides a working girl come to LA.

Then a hard fist slammed into the front door.

"Police. Open up."

# Chapter 6

MY HEART SLAMMED INTO my throat.

I took the three short steps into the living room, and the fist slammed again at the door. I had to get out. "Open up."

The voice wasn't yelling, exactly, but it definitely wanted to be heard.

The voice dropped. "Go ahead, open it up."

Keys jingled on the other side of the door and one was pushed into the lock. I heard it barely, because I was already into the kitchen and at the back door.

I had to hope no copper was out back waiting. I turned the knob and pushed out.

Just as the door into the living room opened.

"Anyone here?" The voice was familiar.

I stepped out through the kitchen door and closed it soft. Then faced with left or right, I headed left back to the back of the property. If there was one cop here, there were most likely more; and if they didn't come busting in, and if he only asked "Anyone here?" when he walked in, chances are he didn't know I was there. I didn't want to take a chance, so I headed around to the back of the property, then let myself out the back gate and into the alley. And I was safe.

For now, anyway.

I headed myself up the alley as fast as I could. The bet was, either head up the alley to the next street before going back to my car, or cut up between the apartment buildings. I figured if a cop saw me coming up from between two buildings, he'd start asking questions; so up to the street it was.

I doubled back around and made it to my car without a problem. Then I started getting curious. Feeling safe at your own car will do that to you. So I took a walk.

A black LAPD Ford was parked outside the bungalows and no other cops were waiting outside with it.

I turned into the bungalows and walked up the center walkway. At the far end, an older woman stood on the steps leading into the back bungalow. The one with the red geranium in the back window.

The woman was plump, white haired, big bosomed, and wore a white and red floral dress that looked like it belonged on a grandmother. I don't know why, but grandmothers always seemed out of place in LA to me. Like a sugar cookie in a speakeasy.

I tipped my hat to the woman, and she gave a soft smile back. A smile ringed in a good amount of confusion.

The steps leading up to bungalow number four had red geraniums planted on either side of them. They matched all the red geraniums planted on either side of all the other bungalows around there. Grandma loved her geraniums.

And I guess loved planting them for people.

I looked back at her again.

You gotta love people who take care of things. Even when the rest of the world didn't give a damn.

The door to number four was closed and the shades still drawn. I couldn't see who was inside, but from the voice before, I had a hunch.

I knocked three quick knocks and stood out on the step with my hat in my hand. Figured the gesture would look better on me.

The door opened.

And there stood Detective Cardon of the LAPD.

Shorter than me by six inches, which meant a slightly below average five feet six he wore the same light brown wool driving cap he always wore. I always thought it made him look like a newsboy on the street.

He was in his early thirties, had a face that looked Midwest open, a nose that had been broken a couple times, had a small scar running from his left eye on toward the back of his head, and green eyes that looked at you like they could see into you. We'd had a few run-ins in the past, and I'd helped him solve a few cases, but usually not before I'd given him a bunch of grief along the way.

All in all, if you saw him walking down the street you might think he was a good egg. And he was.

"Devin." Although the way he said my name made me think he wasn't exactly pleased to see me. Like the proverbial bad penny.

But I like to think of myself more as a dime. "Didn't expect to find you here, Cardon."

"I could say the same." He just stared at me for a bit, his green eyes cutting in to see what they could see. I hoped it wasn't the fact that I'd just been in the bungalow before him.

Cardon and I had gotten off on the wrong foot when I first met him not that long ago. I hadn't been completely honest with him in a case I was working on for a friend. A friend who had died. I had given Cardon enough information to pin four murders in the proper place at the end, but not before being vague enough along the way to let me do my job. Freely.

I think he didn't like me for that. But I did solve the case for him so he got credit, and everything was hunky-dory. At least I hoped.

It was a little odd, though, that he was here. Cops looking to arrest prostitutes usually did it out on the street. They didn't make house calls.

I nodded toward the interior of the bungalow behind Cardon

in the door. "Her name's Holly, the girl who lives here, and I have a client wants to make sure she's okay." I was trying to reach out an olive branch, give him information before he even asked for it.

"Really…" It was a statement more than a question.

"Yeah. How about I come in?"

"No, how about you stay out there."

See, that's what I like about Cardon. He didn't shove me, didn't threaten to arrest me like everyone else on the LAPD, he just stood there like he knew he didn't have to do any of that.

Then he walked out of the door, forcing me down the steps, stopping on the last step as I hit the walkway below. Now he was taller than me. Short guys loved that.

He smiled. "And why are you here, anyway?"

"On the level?"

Cardon almost laughed. "As much as you'll give it to me."

"It's a new year, Cardon. I made resolutions."

Then he did laugh. "To lie only every other word?"

I smiled back, then lowered my voice. The other bungalows were close enough to hear you breathe. "Client hired me, just to check around."

"Who's the client?" He pulled out a small notebook.

"That I can't say."

Cardon looked at me like he was ready to shove me — and arrest me.

"All right, all right. I can't tell you, you know that, but I can tell you what I know. On the level."

He nodded.

I didn't want to talk around the other bungalows so I nodded toward the sidewalk out front. No need to entertain the neighbors.

Out front the street was quiet, one bird calling out somewhere. And it was hot. "Her name is Holly Scanveld. She's a working girl. My client is her… employer."

Cardon looked at me skeptically. "They want their girl back?"

I shook my head. "No. Yes, but… they're actually concerned. My client."

Cardon looked at me, not believing. "I've never met a pimp who was concerned."

"Not a pimp. The woman who runs the house." There, my honesty was showing.

I normally didn't like even giving up that my client was a she, or anything for that matter, but I did decide to be a little more open in the new year. Not spilling things but, maybe being a little more open. I worked alone and while that had done me okay so far, my head wasn't that thick that I could see working with others maybe wasn't going to kill me. "For what it's worth, I believe her."

Cardon nodded.

"She's been missing three days."

There was something in Cardon's eyes, like he'd gone flat.

"What?"

"She was found dead."

It hit me like I didn't want it to. I guess seeing her mom. I guess Rose talking about her the way she did. It got personal and I didn't like that. "Where?"

"In back of a warehouse off of Ninth."

"How?"

Cardon didn't say anything.

I was starting to get mad. "Was it like the others?"

"I can't say anything else."

And that was it, that was all he said.

But there was something else in there, and I was afraid of what it was.

I'd get my own answers.

And I knew the person to get them from.

# Chapter 7

THE BIG GUY DIDN'T think too much, only did what he was told; and what he was told was to grab the girl.

She was pretty, the way most of them were, but this one had black hair and he didn't much care for black hair. Yellow blonde hair, that's what he liked.

He knocked softly on the door of her apartment, like he was told. He stood there next to it, behind him the large brown steamer trunk he had brought. He looked up and down the dark, silent hallway. There was a green rug running all the way up and down it. *Like a Christmas tree*, the big guy thought. That color. He liked it.

But the coast was clear, nobody coming up the hall, and no sounds except a radio coming from the apartment he'd passed on the way up the stairs. That one had a number five on it in a gold number. It was music coming out from there. An orchestra playing the kind of music his ma liked to dance to.

The big guy knocked one more time. He knew she was in there, he watched her walk into the building five minutes ago.

It was noon. He was hungry.

Steps sounded on the other side of the door and they stopped on the other side of him. "Who is it?"

"Me," he answered.

The lock snapped on the other side and the door opened.

The girl looked at him with her head cocked to the side, like she didn't expect to see him here. That was the point.

The big guy slugged her in the face hard, and she fell back into her apartment and hit the floor. She bounced when she hit. Out cold.

The big guy grabbed the handle on the large wardrobe steamer trunk, carried it inside the apartment, closed the door, and strangled the girl right there on the floor before she woke up.

Till she was good and dead.

Then he stuffed her in the trunk, and took her home to do the rest.

# Chapter 8

I MAKE FRIENDS, AND friends help me.

Not the kind of friends that have you over for tea, not the friends who've known you for years. Friends who can do things for you.

Because you did things for them.

Take Bartie James. Now good old Bartie was a nice old guy. Sixty-two, with gray hair on top of his head that he rubbed a lot when he thought. And when he did, you knew there was something running around up in that noggin of his.

So one day Bartie gets it in himself that his wife is out cheating on him. Don't know why. I saw them a lot together down at Toots' place and they seemed happy as clams. They'd laugh, swap stories with Toots, and look like they got on great together. A lot better than me and women.

So one night Bartie's in Toots' and he's rubbing his head like he was hoping a genie would jump out. None did. So I asked him what was up and he told me: his wife was cheating on him.

That didn't make much sense to me, but I'd seen things in my day, so I followed her around a bit.

Turned out she was going to a drawing class. The kind with

27

models, with no clothes on.

Everybody has something.

When I told Bartie, he was so happy he bought a round for the house. And me? I made a new friend.

It's not like I go looking to make friends, it just naturally happens. I look at a person like Bartie and what he's going through — and I don't like it. So I help.

And Bartie? He's helped me a time or two. He's actually a doctor, for dead people. He works at the coroner's.

"Oh, I don't need to check, I remember her. Very well indeed."

We stood outside the Hall of Justice on Temple, its white granite face blinding in the sun. But Bartie liked the outside, so that's where we met. I guess if you spend all day cutting up dead bodies, you don't mind a little air as often as you can get it.

We also stood right out front, which wasn't my idea of keeping things quiet; but Bartie only had a couple minutes. So you make do.

"What about her?"

Bartie looked up at City Hall on the next block. Twenty-seven stories of white rock. The tallest thing in the city. "Did you know the Lindbergh Beacon was a mistake?"

Bartie was always getting distracted. "Bartie, the girl."

He looked back down at me and his eyes locked on and registered, as if seeing me for the first time. "Oh, yes… head and all four limbs severed. With a saw. A wood saw — I could tell it was a wood saw because…"

Holly had died like the others.

Bartie went on talking about the length of saw teeth and the marks they left on skin and bone, but I went to Holly.

I'd seen a lot in my time in Los Angeles — stabbings, gun shots, crushed skulls, all the usuals. But not women getting cut up.

"They say the white light is confusing."

I looked up. "What?"

Bartie was looking back up at the top of the new City Hall, at the Lindbergh Beacon that sat right at the top of the four-sided pyramid that topped the place. The light was installed when the building opened a couple years back. Eight-million-candlepower of light that cuts out and over Los Angeles, rotating once every ten seconds, shooting out a beam of light so every airplane knows it's Los Angeles.

Bartie laughed. "It seems that the light looks like an airport beacon and once an airplane approaches," Bartie waved his hands at all the granite and concrete buildings that stretched up and out around us, "they have no place to land." He smiled. "Land around here, and you die."

Then he laughed.

I didn't laugh. I couldn't. I couldn't help thinking about Holly. And her mother.

And Rose.

Murder left a lot of victims. I wasn't feeling too good.

Bartie still looked up at the beacon that was silent in the light of the day. "She was like the others. I told you that, right?"

No, he hadn't, but I knew. I humored him. "What others?"

"The four others." Bartie looked me right in the eyes, no longer distracted. "This woman you asked about, she was like the others. She is the fifth as a matter of fact. All the same. All sawn up." He said it like a child reciting the end of a nursery rhyme.

It had been all over the papers. They called whoever was doing it The Butcher — whoever *he* was. For the last month, huge headlines screamed out every time a new girl was found. Cut up. I thought of Holly, cut up. And now on the front pages.

I let out a big breath that I hadn't known I was holding. "So all the same?" My mind was still swimming.

"Yes. Same saw, all of them found nude, plus heavy bruises on some. I'm an expert on them all." Then he tilted his head just a bit as he looked at me. "Was your girl a lady of the night?"

Bartie, always proper.

"Yes."

"Then everything is the same. All white, all between the ages of twenty and twenty-five. All quite lovely." Then he looked up at the Lindbergh Beacon again. "There is talk of them turning it to a red light." Then he smiled back at me. "I find that fascinating."

He told me a few other things, when the girls died, where they were dropped, but I had already tuned out. Holly was found. The case was over.

But one thing I learned a long time ago — cases were never over.

Ever.

Until you killed them yourself.

# Chapter 9

I HAD TO LET Rose know Holly was dead. I'd see if she knew anything about Holly's parents, but my guess was that Cardon would find all that out and let them know himself. I'm glad I didn't have to make the call.

I was still shook, and couldn't really focus.

I got to my office fifteen minutes after I left Bartie's, and Bella sat at her desk. Charlie was nowhere. He was probably down in the basement where we kept most of the files.

I felt sorry for the kid — a boy, trying to become a man. And getting his butt kicked by Bella.

But when I was only a little older than him, I was getting my butt kicked by a lot worse. I was already in the Marines and learning to kill. Got my chance at age sixteen in the Great War. 1918. A sunny field in France. It was hot, the grass was short, and I remember the way my bullet tore through the neck of the German kid on the other end of my gun. He wasn't much older than me.

I tried to forget it every day. And most nights, too.

Charlie could wait to grow up. At least as much as a kid kicked out of his own house could.

I nodded quick at Bella as I walked into the outer office and headed straight for my own. I didn't feel much like talking. Bella had other ideas.

"You have a message."

"On my desk?"

"No. It's Nolan."

I stopped. Of course it wasn't on my desk. A rule around here. Whenever Jim called, nothing was written down. Not that I didn't like the guy, I did. But it was... complicated.

"He wants you to stop by."

I hadn't seen Jim in a while. "Did he say what for?"

Bella looked at me like I was simple.

No. Of course he wouldn't say.

Jim ran LA's System, the crime syndicate that ran everything bad in LA, at least if you listened to all the preachers, temperance crazies, and people looking for a soapbox. And a good number of regular citizens of LA. Gambling, booze, women, all of it — at least most of it —organized by the System, and all run by Gentleman Jim Nolan.

My friend.

Kind of.

It was complicated.

"All right." I didn't even take off my hat, didn't go into my office, nothing. Just headed out.

Because when Gentleman Jim called, you went.

# Chapter 10

KNOWING GENTLEMAN JIM WAS a complicated thing. Not complicated as in difficult, just complicated as in… complicated.

He was the head of the System and, as a matter of fact, created it.

He started in New Orleans as a runner for a bordello, then moved up to finally run it. And the gambling that came along with it.

He realized that women were just a by-product, a pleasure item, when the real money was made in gambling. That was his bread and butter. And the booze and the women? Side businesses that complimented the main one. But they still made him a lot of money. Money he liked to protect.

Jim rose up around the same time as Al Capone, especially once Prohibition hit. Anything people can't get their hands on legally makes it that much more fun, and that much more profitable for people like Jim.

But where Al operated freely on the streets of Chicago and was brutal about it, Jim decided that he'd put an organization in place that would feed everyone all along the way. Things were handled in a genteel way. Not that there weren't killings, but the idea was to keep things quiet, keep things greased. And everyone would get rich along the way. From beat cops to madams, district attorneys to chiefs of police, from the mayor all the way down to the boys who rolled the barrels of beer. Everyone made money.

The only thing Prohibition did was create the organizations that ran the crime. And in the vast scheme of things, the System's way was a lot better in my book than Capone's way.

And how did I even know Jim? I saved his son Tommy's life. In France. Not long after I killed my first German.

Funny that. You kill one day, and save on another.

That's life, I guess.

The only thing is, Jim seems to think he owes me something for saving Tommy. I keep telling him it was random, that anyone else would have done the same thing, but he won't listen. Keeps throwing me jobs now and then. To help me pay the expenses.

As I pulled up to the large white clapboard house on Hollywood Boulevard, everything looked normal outside. Which means it looked like any other house converted to a business in the area.

A large wraparound porch sat in the front of the place where an accountant had an office, but my business was around in back.

I walked along the small concrete walkway to the back, past a spread of red roses at the base of the house. They loved the California sun, and I guess I did, too.

At the back of the house, I found the simple white back door with no windows, but a small peephole cut in the center.

I knocked on the door, lightly, and open it came, complete with a guy on the other side of it. His one hand still held the doorknob, the other held a Thompson machine gun.

"Devin." The guy smiled and let me in. His head was round like a melon but looked like it was made of granite. Tiny ears poked out from under his brown hat. His brown striped suit jacket strained at the shoulders and his face was split by a crooked nose draped between large green eyes. He was easily in his late thirties.

"Afternoon, Blinky." I had no idea why he was called Blinky and I had never thought to ask. "He in?"

"Yeah, go on up."

The small vestibule held one empty chair, Blinky's, and one occupied by a younger version of Blinky, even bigger but smarter looking. He never said a thing but I knew his name was Bats. I wasn't sure if that referred to his baseball ability or his mental state. Or his favorite tool of choice when dealing with friends of Mr. Nolan. Jim Nolan was gentle. The guys working for him were anything but.

I nodded at Bats. He didn't even acknowledge me, just kept staring down at his own Colt 1911 as if it were the Sunday paper.

Between the two chairs was a simple set of stairs that led up to another closed door, and another guy standing there in front of it. Sean, and Sean had a Thompson, too.

I got to the top of the stairs, nodded to Sean, and he cracked the door to Jim's office.

Probably the most protected place in all of LA.

# Chapter 11

THE OFFICE WAS FULL of light.

A bank of five windows cut into smaller panes lined the far wall, the harsh LA light coming in, throwing Jim into a kind of half shadow as he sat at his desk in front of it. "John, so good of you to come." There was the slightest lilt of Irish still in his voice.

Tommy told me once he used to hear his dad in the bathroom every morning when he woke, and every day before he went to bed, working on his accent as he looked at himself in the mirror.

Jim worked hard to fit in, according to Tommy, and I guess in one way he had. By running all crime in LA.

The room was twenty by twenty, Jim's only nod to his status. Everything else was simple, right down to the simple metal desk he ran things from. Jim got up to come to me.

He stood a thin and lean five foot ten, with gray peppering his black hair and an easy smile that was quick and gentle. It was hard reconciling the man in front of me with what I also knew him to be; gentle as a sleeping cobra.

"How are you, Jim?"

He reached out his hand and grabbed mine. His hand was soft. "It's been too long, John."

"I know."

"Sit down, please."

I picked one of the matching burgundy leather chairs in front of his desk, and as I turned to sit, I saw the two regulars sitting at the burgundy leather sofa against the back wall.

Jake and Easy. They were like a matched set of jagged mountains, only Jake had a snowy-blond top and Easy's head was bald as a windswept boulder. Neither of them wore a hat but both had Thompsons between their legs, stocks down and muzzles up. Their apparent manliness always at attention.

"Boys," I nodded.

Easy didn't move but Jake croaked out, "Devin," before he cracked his neck, rotated his shoulders once, and then went back to staring at the floor.

I sat and turned back around to Jim behind his simple desk.

I felt like a kid at the feet of a king.

The room was completely quiet. Jim took a slow, calm breath and let it out just as slow. When he finished, he looked at me. "I was at his grave yesterday."

Tommy was dead. Five years ago in an attack, with a bullet that was really meant for Jim.

I think Jim never forgave himself after that. So he maybe wanted to treat me like Tommy somehow. So he kept an eye on me.

I didn't say anything back to him. I just nodded and let him have his time.

Jim tapped the desk in front of him softly with one hand like he wasn't sure what to say himself. The room was silent as both of us looked at the green blotter with the black leather corners in front of him. Then the patting stopped. "Right, then." He looked up at me with his easy smile. "How are things for you, John?"

I never really got used to people calling me John. I was so used to people calling me Devin. The only person who ever called me John was my mother, and she had been dead for years. My father had only ever called me asshole. "Going along okay."

"You need any money or anything? Shame about the market,

did you have any money in it?"

"Me? No. I don't have enough to play, and if I did, I wouldn't. I figure the odds are stacked against you."

Jim nodded.

"But everything is fine."

"Any girl?"

I laughed. "No girl."

"That's a shame, John. Lizzie and me have been married thirty years now. Celebrated just last month."

"Congratulations. Tell her I said hello."

The last time I had seen Lizzie was at Tommy's funeral. I never want to see a crushed mother again. That made me think of what Holly's mother was about to go through.

That made me feel not so good again.

"I will." Jim patted the blotter in front of him. "Well then, on to business. I'd like to hire you, John."

"Sure thing, what do you need?"

"And this is to remain confidential."

"Absolutely."

"Good, then. We've had some problems with girls at the bordellos."

It was a curious word, and an old word to use. I'd heard them called everything from whorehouse to cathouse to... worse, but "bordellos" was positively ancient. I guessed it had more to do with how he'd come up in the world.

"Four of them have been, how shall I say, murdered."

I couldn't imagine a man like Jim having trouble saying a word like murder.

"And savagely. Their heads and arms and legs cut off."

"Four?"

"Four."

I debated whether to tell him he had a fifth, too, in Holly.

But I definitely wasn't going to tell him Rose had come to me already. If I needed to tell him, I would. "I'll need their names." I'd cross-check those names against the names that Bartie had.

"Get them from Carlo. You'll be meeting with him after we're done. He got to the hotel early so he could give you what you needed."

That wasn't good.

Carlo Genovese was not a man to wake up before five in the evening. He was like a stick of dynamite with an eighth-inch fuse, and he didn't like me to begin with. We'd had a few run-ins along the way and I'm sure he wasn't going to be happy to see me.

Unfortunately, he was one of Jim's lieutenants and ran the whole prostitution end of the System. The faster I could get away from him, the better.

"This has all been unfortunate. I wouldn't normally bother you with this, but it's more than my men are capable of... handling. News travels fast with the girls, and after the first two were killed, they were scared and that was no problem. Then after the third, some of them started to refuse to work. They said it wasn't safe. Then after the fourth, a lot of them stopped completely. So — business has stopped."

"I understand."

Jim looked around the room like there was something more and he didn't want to get into it.

Then he did.

"The only other thing I'd like to add, John, is," Jim looked his hazel eyes right at me, "you can of course let me know once you find out who is doing this to me, and I will send someone to take care of him. But, if you'd like to take care of him yourself, I will pay you a bonus. But I know this is something you may not want to do."

It was always complicated with Jim.

"I appreciate the offer Jim." But I didn't. I didn't want to get wrapped up in that side of things.

I think he wanted to help me after what I had done for Tommy. But how he tried, always created a little tension whenever I was near him.

Back in school they always talked about planets, and how they

39

pulled on each other. These big, huge balls in the black sky pulling on each other. And how the moon pulls on the Earth, and makes the oceans try to come to it.

I felt that way when I came to see Jim sometimes. That there was this huge weight sitting there on the other side of a simple, gray metal desk. I only knew him as the father of a friend who was killed, but the rest of the city knew him, or really didn't know him, as the leader of all that was bad in LA. And in a way, I felt that pull, like even an entire ocean can feel itself being pulled.

Like I say, with Jim it was complicated.

But for Tommy, I would help him.

And I could still keep things separate. Jim, the father of an old buddy, my only buddy, and Jim, the man in front of everything else.

"I'll find him, Jim."

"You do that."

Jim got up from his desk, came around to the front, and shook my hand.

His hand was soft. And it wasn't made of iron.

I looked behind the desk and Jim's chair, and on the ledge of the window behind it was a picture of Tommy. Maybe when he was ten. He stood at the edge of the ocean, in front of the waves crashing in back of him. The smile on his face was full of life.

I looked back at Jim, into his hazel eyes, and he looked tired.

I thought he maybe needed to get down to the ocean himself.

I always felt better when I did.

"I'll find him, Jim."

Jim nodded, and I left.

And I had a very empty feeling about all of this. I didn't know why.

Soon, I would.

# Chapter 12

THE SANTORINI ARMS WAS a small rooming house a half mile off the ocean in Venice Beach.

A relatively new building, it looked more like an apartment building. It was a two story box with flat windows stuck onto it, and the whole thing painted a bright yellow that was either supposed to remind you of sunshine, or a lemon.

To me it just stuck out like a lemon. And that seemed to be what you didn't want for a house of prostitution, especially if you were a part of the System. But Carlo was flashy, he liked his attention. And I never figured out just why, or how, Jim would have ever gotten mixed up with a guy like this.

But they had known each other back in New Orleans. I guess in any kind of business like this, you take the devil you know.

The day was hot but I could smell the freshness of the breeze blowing in off the ocean. It was always ten degrees cooler over here and I kept forgetting just how much that little bit can mean in a city as hot as LA. It was downright pleasant.

I walked through the beating sun and up the drive to the side entrance. Just as I reached for the handle of the door, a scratchy voice boomed out from above. "Devin. About time. Get up here."

Carlo. And it was just like him to turn an order from Jim into his own for me to get up there. I could tell this was going to be real sweet.

The entrance to the place had a small booth cut out of the wall opposite the door. Inside sat a big guy wearing a tan striped shirt and a shoulder holster. He was in his early thirties, his neck was thick, and even though he was sitting, he looked taller than me. All in all big, and probably Carlo's muscle, which meant he probably didn't speak.

He barely looked at me, then went back to the paper sitting on the counter in front of him. I imagined he had to sound out the words.

The stairs were sharp and narrow, and at the top I rapped on the first door to my right, a white one with no number painted on it. The other doors that I saw down the bright hall did have numbers, painted on them in black. They actually looked professional.

I knocked on the door again.

"Get in here."

I opened the door.

Inside, the apartment was bright, two windows cut into the far wall. In front of one of them stood a guy I recognized as Vince, no nickname. He was small, wiry, bald, and the same height as Carlo. Which meant five-six if he was wearing lifts. But what Vince lacked in height, he more than made up for in meanness. He rarely talked, and did most of Carlo's "legwork."

Carlo stood in front of the other window, a kitchen table and matching chromium and blue chairs between them.

Carlo was short like Vince but he was solid. He had short-cropped black hair ending in a widow's peak in front, and black whiskers that covered everything else. All in all — he looked like a stocky monkey.

And that made me smile.

He wore a black suit with a gaudy yellow tie that matched the paint on the outside of the building. He held a cigarette to his mouth, his hand like a fist, with a large pinky ring that looked like a gold nugget draping off of it. His shoes were orangish-brown and all flash, complete with built-up soles meant for nothing other than to push their occupant taller into the air. They looked stupid. "So you're on the case, huh, dick?"

Carlo was framed by the window, the light coming in from behind making him look almost black. Maybe he just sucked the light out of everything. I liked that thought better. "Look, Carlo, I don't want to be here any more than you want me here. Just give me the names of the four girls and I'll be out of your hair."

Carlo smiled, a wicked smile, and sat down at the table. Vince followed suit. Then Carlo nodded to a small sheet of white paper sitting on the table in front of him. "They're right there." His teeth flashed white in his mean little mouth. "Come and get 'em."

I walked to the table, the white sheet of paper sitting plain on top of the blue tabletop. It was a small piece of notebook paper, no lines, just plain white with four lines of black scratches on it. Four names and addresses, jagged-written, like something caught between hate and rage.

I reached out to pick it up from the top. I had my hand nearly there when a switchblade arced down like a hammer, Carlo slamming it into the page right next to my thumb.

The switchblade's edge sliced just a fraction into my skin.

I didn't flinch.

I pulled the piece of white notebook paper out, right through the blade of the knife.

The blade was sharp and the paper slipped out easily, whole at the bottom and sliced clean up toward the top. The two sides on either side of the split floated down limp and slashed.

I carefully folded the loose halves down onto the whole half at the bottom, then folded it one more time to lock them in. Then I slipped the note into my inside jacket pocket. I felt the butt of one of my guns as I did, and would have loved to have smashed Carlo's face with it. Would have loved it a lot.

When I pulled my hand out, a small bit of blood caught at the edge of the lapel of my jacket. My suit was dark blue, so that wasn't a problem; the problem was the white pinstripes. My blood smeared across a couple of them.

I looked down at the stain, then up at Carlo.

He wasn't even smiling.

Dead. That was his eyes. And I could see them now that I was closer. They tried to be the darkest brown imaginable but they didn't make it. They were black.

The black of death.

"One other thing." Carlo put out his cigarette in a thick, round glass ashtray that was filled almost to the top with butts. "You're going to talk to a girl here."

"Really?" I was getting tired of being told what to do.

"Yeah, really. A guy tried to take her."

"When?"

"Couple weeks back."

That would have been in the middle of all of this. The other girls had been found over the last month.

Carlo nodded over Vince's shoulder. "She's in the room next door." Carlo took out and lit another cigarette, and blew smoke toward my face. "We kept her out of rotation until you got here. Make it quick, she's got things to do." His mouth crooked up at one end, I suppose trying to make a smile. It didn't work.

I left.

I wanted the hell out of there.

# Chapter 13

IF PROSTITUTES CAME IN flavors, Eula was a mouse.

Her hair looked like it, her brown eyes darted, and in the smallness of her body, she sat like someone was going to attack her at any minute. It wasn't going to be me. I only wanted answers.

Vince stood in the doorway while Carlo leaned against the wall inside the room, keeping an eye on Eula.

Eula sat on the iron bed in the middle of the room, wearing a light blue cotton blouse on top, and deeper blue skirt below. The blouse had long sleeves and the skirt was long, too. Pretty covered up for a prostitute, I thought, but then again, some guys liked it.

The room was like any other prostitute's room — bare, plain, with the bed and, lucky for Eula, a window. Light shone in through it.

"What did the guy look like?"

She didn't answer, but kept looking up at Carlo, like she was worried she'd say or do something he didn't want.

That took me back.

My mother and the old man would do this. I immediately felt uncomfortable, a small, strangled feeling coming up into my throat. It took me back to a place I did not want to go. "Look,

Eula, I'm trying to get the guy. Jim Nolan himself hired me. He's worried about all of you." He was actually more worried about his business, but I figured a little white lie wouldn't matter that much. Besides, a powerful urge to get the hell out of there started knocking on my door.

It was always that way when I saw two people like this.

"Tell him." Carlo said it to Eula with a threat. Then he looked at me and nodded toward Eula. "She's scared of the guy."

From the way Eula looked at Carlo, seemed like to me she was scared of more than just the guy that attacked her.

Finally Eula started. "He was big. That's all I know. And I don't remember anything else. But he was definitely there. Definitely was." She looked at Carlo, wondering if she did okay.

I didn't know what was going on. It was as if the whole thing was rehearsed, with Carlo standing over Eula, threatening, making sure she said exactly what he wanted.

But there was also something in Eula's eyes that I see. It was something focused not on the two guys in the room with us, but on something else entirely. Something else she had seen — and lived through.

I think there really was a guy. "I promise you, Eula, I will get this guy and he will never come after you again."

She looked up at me, her brown mouse eyes reaching up to me like she wanted to believe what I was saying. That reminded me of the way my mother looked sometimes. Like she wanted to believe that everything would be all right.

"Okay," I began, "let's just start with what happened. You can do that for me, Eula, right? Just tell me what happened."

Eula looked up, the softness in her eyes flipping to something much harder. "You're gonna kill him, right? That's what Gentleman Jim wants you to do, right?" The mouse turning into a lion.

I looked Eula straight in the eyes. "The guy won't do it again."

Something shifted in her; maybe she did believe me. She began playing with a crease in her blue skirt like a child worried at a piece of thread. "I got home from work, was opening my door and I heard something from behind. I moved out of the way, but his arm came around me and got me around the head. I think he was trying for the throat and missed on account of I moved. I'm quick that way. So he had his arm, a big arm and strong, around my head and crushing it. Then he moved it over my mouth — so I bit him, hard. He loosened right up and then I screamed. Screamed and screamed as hard as I could. Then he hit me with something and I went out. The next thing I knew, I was lying on the floor outside my door with three neighbors standing over me. The big guy was gone."

"Did you call the cops?"

She laughed at me with thin lips. "Are you kidding? You think I want anything to do with them?"

So Cardon didn't know about her. "What did he look like?"

"Like I say, I didn't see nothin'. Just felt him behind me. And when he shifted his arm to my mouth, I saw a black hat out the corner of my eye." She looked me up and down. "He was bigger than you. And he had a puffy face. Like he ate too much."

"Fat?"

She started to get angry. "Like I say — I didn't see him."

Seemed like she saw enough to me, but I backed off. "Has he been back?"

Eula smiled a bit. "I don't know, I been here ever since." She looked up at Carlo.

"You're staying here?"

Carlo broke in, his chest pumped up. "I wanted to take care of her. Didn't I, Eula?"

She looked up at him like a kid looks up at a father, and again, the strangled feeling came back up to my throat.

"When did the big guy come after you?"

"Two weeks ago."

It would fit with the timing of the other girls. According to Bartie, the first girl was found a month ago. The next one, five days after that.

Light continued to show in through the window, and I could

hear the distant thumping of a bed headboard against a wall.

There was no moaning.

"Thanks for your time."

Eula just sat there in the bed as I walked out, I imagine waiting for her next customer.

As I walked to my car, I thought about what I had so far and there wasn't much. A big guy. At least if Eula was to be believed, and I really didn't have any reason to doubt her. Even if Carlo was watching over her like a hawk.

But still, that part bothered me. Him.

Of course that was just ghosts of the past, my mother and the old man. Better to push that back down and lock the door up tight. So I focused on the case and felt the anger rise up in me. But anger at what?

Maybe it was what happened to Holly. Or what I saw happening between Carlo and Eula.

Or maybe it was what was behind that door inside me that I kept locked up tight.

But either way, it was okay because anger always had a way of burning through things.

When I was angry, I got to the truth.

Quick.

# Chapter 14

CARLO STOOD, WALKING AROUND his room in the Santorini. It's how he did his thinking. Like a caged lion.

And he wanted to hit something, bad.

"I don't want Devin looking into this any deeper than he has to, and I don't care if Jim got him. You know what I mean?"

Vince looked up from the small table.

An energetic customer was already driving into the bed springs in the room next door. Eula's room.

Carlo looked at the wall between, with a small print of a mountain scene set into a cheap frame. The muffled banging kept coming through the wall, rhythmic. Then a muffled cry came through. Eula's.

Carlo kept staring at the wall. "You go, see what he's doing. If he starts getting too close, let me know; but if you need to do something, do it. I'll handle Jim."

Vince nodded once, then got to his feet and headed to the door.

Carlo kept looking at the wall. His mouth had gone dry and he could only think of one thing. "Tell Sal nobody else for Eula for a while."

Carlo had some things to work off.

# Chapter 15

I GOT BACK INTO Holly's with no problem.

I shut the back door like I had the first time, and this time I hoped I wouldn't be interrupted. The shade on the back door was up now so I pulled it down. I didn't know if anyone was going to be walking up and down the back of the place like I was, but no sense taking chances.

The kitchen looked the same as the first time. Small, tight, and compact.

The only thing that was different was that the water from the overflowing drain pan under the icebox had been cleaned up, and the floor looked like it had been mopped. Probably the old lady with the red geranium in the end bungalow. She was probably the manager of the place, and maybe getting it ready to rent out again.

I was hoping I would find something to help me out. It seemed from the first time I'd been here that Holly was pretty thorough herself — in hiding any trace of who and what she was. It was almost too clean, like maybe there was too much to hide.

As in the place was empty.

I decided to start in the bedroom.

I walked out into the small living room with the two chairs

against the wall and the white table-clothed table with the radio on it. The photo of her mother was gone, I guessed Cardon had taken that. I wondered if there was anything on the back, some kind of clue. Anything.

The window shades were up, the light streaming in from outside. Not great. I stood in the doorway from the kitchen, looking out through the one window facing out to the courtyard and the other bungalow facing it. Nobody seemed to be around so I walked very slow, my movements steady, and kept to the far wall.

I felt like a burglar, which I guess I was. But I wasn't there to steal anything, just find anything I could on Holly.

I got to the bedroom on the other side of the living room and got myself inside.

It was darker in there. Only one window, and that faced to the north, and its shade was down.

The small iron bed was still there but had had the sheets stripped. The mattress was thin, made out of a tough white cotton with light blue stripes in it. I recognized the type from my own place. The blue and white stripes reminded me of a train engineer's coveralls. Funny, that.

The small, dark wood side table still sat next to the bed, as did the matching dark wood chest of drawers at the end of the bed. On top of the chest of drawers now was a box, filled with clothes and things.

I was sure Cardon had already been through those, so I thought I'd start with everything else.

I pulled the mattress off the bed and laid it on the floor, then pulled the frame up and on its end so I could check everything underneath.

There was no dust under the bed, and I wondered if that was Holly being clean or the old woman doing a good job. With as clean as the rest of the place was, I figured it was Holly.

A quick check of the frame revealed nothing, and a long pat-down of the mattress revealed the same. Nothing.

I put the mattress back on the frame, then pulled out the

two empty drawers from the side table, and checked each one for anything on the backs or undersides. Nothing. Then I did a quick check of the insides where the drawers sat. Again, nothing.

I was coming up dry, but ninety-nine percent of what I do is coming up dry, so I've gotten used to it. But I also do something else most other people forget: I trust that something will come.

I don't know if it's a gift I have, but a lot of other people have quit right when they were about to… get what they wanted.

I pulled the empty drawers from the chest of drawers and checked those, then checked what was in the box. Assorted women's clothes, odds and ends like a half-worn pencil and a cheap dime novel about love. That hit me strange, the novel. But I guess it shouldn't, everyone wanted love. Even a prostitute.

I checked the floor for any boards out of place, checked the baseboards along the wall and anything along the ceiling. Anything that looked like it could hide something. I pulled and pushed, got down on my knees and squinted up into corners, including inside the small closet. Nothing.

The living room was the same, after I lowered the shades. I even checked inside the radio, a very popular place to hide things. Nothing.

The bathroom was next. It was small with six-sided, white tiles on the floor, one window, a toilet, sink, and bathtub. And one used bar of white soap that sat on the sink.

A quick sweep of the floor, the inside of the toilet tank, and the underside of the sink revealed nothing. Above the sink was a white wooden medicine cabinet mounted flush into the wall, with a small bit of wood trim around the four sides to finish it off. Which was nice. I'd seen my share of places, including my own, where the cabinet was mounted on top of the wall so that it stuck out and away from it. As in the perfect place to smack your head when you've been rinsing your face in the sink and come up to see if you got everything.

I've had enough times where I forgot it was there and nearly took my head off when I came up. Well, my head is pretty hard, so actually it was more like I almost took the cabinet off the wall.

I swung open the cabinet door with the mirror in the middle and looked inside.

It had two white shelves, with the bottom of the cabinet providing a third. Nothing sat on the top two shelves but on the bottom of the cabinet were a few pots of makeup, one black tube of lipstick, a role of bandaging, and a clear bottle of mercurochrome. The bottle was half-filled, its white label stained with the red liquid that had dropped down the side of the bottle.

I took out each of the makeup pots and the lipstick, opened each, and looked inside. Women's things, and nothing out of the ordinary. But as I moved the rest around a bit, something else caught my eye.

Tucked in the bottom edges of the cabinet, hidden behind the pots and bottles and the bandaging, were two nails. One on each side, driven into the edge where the left and right sides of the cabinet met the bottom of it.

Now there was nothing out of the ordinary about the nails being there. They were hammered in to anchor the cabinet to the wall studs on either side of the cabinet. Nothing like opening the mirrored door and having the thing fall right out of the hole cut into the wall. So nails are perfectly normal.

But what wasn't normal were the heads. They were squeezed and crushed like they had been bitten with teeth. And the exposed, crushed edges of the metal were bright like they were new, or, like they had been recently bitten — with plyers.

I stuck my fingers to pull them out but they were seated in pretty tight.

I had a hunch, went to the kitchen and checked below the sink. Sure enough, in the back corner was a new hammer, and lying next to it, a new set of pliers — complete with a good set of teeth. And those teeth looked like they could bite into the heads of a certain couple of nails.

I went back into the bathroom, pulled at the nails, and they came out easy enough. Then I pulled the cabinet out of the hole in the wall.

Inside the hole was mostly what I expected to see. Facing me was the plaster and lath that made up the wall on the other side. And on either side of the hole were two honey-brown, rough wall studs that the cabinet was fitted between. At the bottom of the space was a small horizontal board fitted between the two studs, giving the cabinet something to rest on. The carpenter had done a good job. But there was one more thing. A very out-of-place finishing nail was driven into the back of the horizontal support board. It had nothing to do with the cabinet but everything to do with a single piece of dusty white string tied to it, the string falling behind the support board and on down the inside of the wall.

I reached in and pulled the white string, and from below the support board came the end of the string — a tiny silver key attached to it.

It wasn't a house key, it was a key to a lock. A very specific type of lock. And how did I recognize it?

Because I had two of them myself. And I knew exactly where that key belonged.

I was finally in business.

# Chapter 16

THERE ARE KEYS FOR a lot of things in this world.

Keys for locks, keys for automobiles, and keys for homes. And Holly's key fit none of them.

Central Station was one of two train stations in Los Angeles. It had a federal style that looked like it could have come straight out of Washington, D.C., and was the only station in town to handle the Southern Pacific line.

Inside, the grand hall at its center rose up thirty feet to the ceiling, the noise of two hundred people milling around inside bouncing off the marble walls like gunshots through a canyon. You could barely hear yourself think.

A large, white marble counter stood to my left as I walked in, with large doors on the opposite wall that led out to the tracks beyond. Brass bells clanged and a great hiss of steam sounded from the other side of the doors as a great locomotive passed on the tracks beyond.

Light flooded into the great hall from five massive windows, while eight large Victorian chandeliers hung from the ceiling on black chains. Even during the day, the chandeliers were lit, each with eight white globes of light mounted onto their circular frame.

Eight was an odd number. The only place I'd known eight to be liked was in China. It was a lucky number, a prosperous number. I wondered if all the Chinese who laid the track around here had somehow had a hand in designing the chandeliers. I doubted it.

So somehow somebody got lucky, and chose a lucky number when designing it.

I hoped I was lucky in what I came here to find.

I headed right, toward one end of the great hall, where a large corridor headed into the next wing of the place. A carved wood ceiling ran along the corridor with shops on either side, but where I headed was a small, at least for this place, room with a large arched entry into it. Twenty feet deep by forty feet long, the room was lined along all the walls with small metal boxes.

Lockers.

"Devin…"

I smiled. "Hi, Billie."

Billie was a kid about eighteen who came up to the middle of my chest. Which basically meant he was five feet tall. Sandy brown hair stuck off at all angles and he had a smile that wouldn't quit. And freckles. A lot of them. Five feet and freckles, he probably never heard the end of it, which is why I was always surprised he had a smile on his mug instead of a big old stick you.

"You here for one of your lockers?"

"Actually no, Billie. Here for someone else's."

"Oh." Billie's green eyes looked at me with a question.

He wore the navy blue shirt and pants of a Southern Pacific porter, but his official job was tending the new key-operated storage lockers at the station. A new invention, replacing a desk and a person behind it, the new lockers were simple: pick a locker, put in a dime, take your key, and you're done.

The normal time to leave your bag, or whatever else you wanted to leave, was two days. But it was a pretty well-known secret that if you got friendly with the attendant, Billie in this case, and slipped him a little something for his troubles, you could keep things there — until you needed them.

Holly wasn't going to be able to come back for whatever was inside her locker but I figured I needed it. If I was lucky, it might just lead me to whoever killed her.

I kept thinking about the eight white globes on the eight chandeliers out front and thought of good luck. I even kept saying *dójeh* in my head. That's Chinese for "thank you." I figured it couldn't hurt.

I pulled the key from my pocket and already knew the number, 134. I headed to the back wall, found the hundreds, then found 134. One row off the bottom. A tan locker about one foot by one foot.

Billie followed me and watched as I put the key in the lock. "Miss Anderson's locker."

So Holly used a different last name when she talked with Billie. I wasn't surprised. You didn't use a locker to be known, you used it to keep things safe. Like a safe deposit box — for people who couldn't use a bank.

I swung the small tan door open and inside were two shoe boxes, both tied with string. One, the smaller, in front, was yellow. The one in back was black. I figured there weren't shoes in either one of them.

It was a funny thing and I could never quite understand it, but women could not have bank accounts on their own. At least single women. Men had to start them, and if you didn't have a husband or a brother in town to start one for you, you were pretty much out of luck.

Which is why I was there at the train station, looking at the only safe place Holly felt she could leave something.

Billie stood near me, watching, not knowing if he should try to stop me or not. I figured he was old enough. "She's dead, Billie."

Billie's head snapped to the left a bit, like something hit him. "How?"

"Someone killed her. I'm trying to find out who."

Billie stood there, I suppose, wondering what to do. Technically now, what was in the locker, was the property of Southern Pacific.

Or whoever wanted to take it first. Maybe the attendants did their share of it, but who was to know? But I hoped Billie was better than that. I thought he was. There might be a few honest people in the world, but not a lot of them were located here in Los Angeles.

Billie nodded toward the locker. "You think there might be something in there, to help you?" I saw a tear form up at the inside of his right eye.

Eighteen, and maybe never had anyone die around him. He seemed like a kid you wanted to protect. "That's what I'm hoping, Billie."

He pulled out a ring of keys and walked a little ways down the line to a storage locker three rows up from the bottom. He put the key in, twisted it in the lock, then opened the small door the same size as the one I was already in. He didn't look inside but nodded toward it. "This is another one of hers. Maybe that might have something, too."

Then he turned and walked out through the small arch that lead out of the room. I figured he was going to get a drink of water.

Or something.

I left the first locker and walked over to the second. Inside was a single white envelope. The business kind. There was nobody else in the room, so I pulled the envelope out and opened it.

It was photos. A dozen of them. And the first one, the one on top, was of Holly lying naked on a bed, arms and feet tied to all four corners. A bald guy stood on the far side of the bed, really tall, his arm blurred in motion as his fist came down fast toward her left thigh. In the photo, the fist was almost at her bare thigh.

I felt gut-punched.

I flashed through a couple of the other snaps and it was more of the same, girls getting hit. My breath got shorter and angrier. The men doing the hitting were all different, except the tall bald guy hitting Holly in the first snap. He was in five — almost half — of them. All hitting Holly.

The bruises, the hitting, all I could think about was my mother.

I quick-shoved the snaps back in the envelope, shaking. Then

I shoved the rage back inside me, deep, where it always seemed to live.

I put the white envelope inside my jacket pocket, then walked back to the first locker and got the two shoe boxes out. The yellow box was light, the black box was heavy, and both were tied with the same white string that held the key back in Holly's bathroom.

I was afraid to look in either of the boxes to see what else I would find, so I decided to get the hell out of there pronto. Out in the Grand Hall, there were probably two hundred people who crowded the place. Everyone jostling, everyone pushing, everyone living their lives without a care in the world.

And none of them even knew Holly existed. Or used to exist.

Past tense.

I wanted to kill someone.

# Chapter 17

BY THE TIME I made it back to my office it was dark — and that was good. I could go through the boxes by myself. No interruptions.

I had also cooled off a little. A little.

It was quiet as I entered the outer office. Bella's desk was neat as it always was and that made me think of the kid. Charlie didn't have a place in the office, he just kind of floated around.

Not that he needed a place. After all, I had gotten him a room at the Trudy Motel because his old man had kicked him out of the house. At least it was a roof over his head. But without a place, you can feel not grounded. When I was Charlie's age I had my own little place, a workbench in the barn that I could call my own.

I kept that thing clean. It was mine.

By the time of my last summer at the farm, I was sixteen and three inches taller than the old man. We had worked out an unsaid agreement that I would keep to the barn and fix the equipment and machines, while he would stay inside the house and wouldn't come out to the barn except when he pulled in with the tractor. It was best that way. Until one time when he was inside the house. Mom's screams were pretty loud and I came in running.

I landed one punch, and then he took an axe handle to me. Doctor said I was lucky.

The old man told him I'd fallen from the hay loft.

My mom couldn't stop shaking, and made me promise not to do anything like it again. A few days later, she gave me money she had saved and told me to get away. Told me to go to her brother. She was afraid. Afraid for what I might do, and afraid for what the old man might do back.

She made me promise to write to Mrs. Brinson next door, let her know where I was. I made her promise to leave soon herself.

I left on the 5th of July, 1918.

I didn't go to her brother, I had another idea.

After the Great War started in 1917, there was a poster up in the post office. It had to be the most amazing thing I had ever seen. It was dark yellow and had the face of a guy in uniform on it. Big. And a rifle cutting across it like he was ready to use it. I just wanted to use an axe handle. I wanted to be strong, and learn how to fight. So I joined that guy on the poster. He was a Marine. And I was going to learn how to kill Germans, and then come back and rip that axe handle away from the old man. Then I'd teach him how it could really be used.

When I walked into my dark office it was stuffy. Bella had closed all the windows against any rain that might end up coming. She could have saved herself the trouble. It never rained in LA.

I dropped the two shoe boxes on the green blotter on top of my desk, then opened all three windows into the place. The breeze blew in but it wasn't going to be near enough. I switched on the two desk lights on either side of my desk, then turned on the fan that sat to the left on the desk. Instantly, I felt the breeze sweep out. That would help.

I took off my hat and jacket, hung them on the coat rack behind me, and pulled out a bottle of cheap stuff from my desk drawer, along with a rocks glass. I preferred drinking alone. It saved on conversation.

I sat down and poured and drank fast, the sharp burn raking

me all the way down. Maybe I should go to Toots'. At least there I would get the good stuff.

But I kept seeing Holly. Not the nice picture Rose brought me, but the one I saw from the envelope still in my pocket. It was actually heavy in there. Maybe with all the girls, and all the sons of bitches hitting them.

I couldn't face them all yet — so I went for the two shoe boxes.

I pulled the yellow one to me and untied the white string that held it tight.

Inside there were things… memories, really. Like what a kid would hold underneath his bed. His entire life in a box.

A baptismal handkerchief, small and white, lay to one side. I recognized it because I had seen mine once. Spilling down from the handkerchief were some colorful buttons, and at the bottom of the small box were some sheaves of miscellaneous paper. But sitting on top of the paper at the bottom and just below the handkerchief and buttons, was a small poster for a picture that looked like it was directed by Busby Berkeley. "Broadway Review" it said across the top, in bold red letters rimmed in bright yellow. There was a picture of a girl on the front, all blonde and happy, and in the background was a dancing line. I couldn't make Holly out in any of the faces in the dancing line, but I wondered if this was one of the pictures that Rose mentioned. Had to be. Holly's claim to fame. Her success.

I never understood all these people coming to LA by the trainload. There were a lot of people with dreams out east and they all seemed to come here, west.

The odds didn't seem that high for me, though. It was hard to break into the pictures. Me? I just wanted three squares a day and a place to sleep. Maybe that's all any of us wanted in the end, but some always wanted a little more. I guess Holly wanted more.

But I couldn't blame the kid for trying. I was trying every day to keep a detective business running and here she was actually in a picture. More than a lot of other people out there could say. I wondered if Holly realized that, that she actually had done good.

She'd gotten away from wherever it was she left. I suppose there were other ways of making a living out there but...

I thought back to the photos. No. I was sorry she came out here.

The rest of the box contained nothing much interesting. The memories of a girl. The only thing was she didn't keep them in her apartment, though, and that seemed a little odd.

But you do that if you don't feel safe.

I wondered how much in danger she knew she was.

I thought about the pictures in their white envelope and wasn't sure if Holly was the blackmailing type, but there are all kinds of reasons she might have them. Maybe it was for money, maybe it was for insurance.

Maybe she was tired of the life and just wanted to get out. It's a hard racket to get out of. And maybe she needed a little leverage.

I opened the other box, the larger black one, and it was filled with money. A lot of it. All in thick stacks. All placed long-ways across the box and it just fit the bills. Like it was made for them.

I pulled the money out, five and a half stacks. Singles, fives, and tens. A few twenties floated at the bottom of everything like a thin carpet. I counted it all up and there was exactly $1,576.

I thought about it and wondered how long Holly had had to save up to get all this. How many... hits it represented. How many bruises. Maybe that's why she did it all, to bank the dough and get out. With the photos as insurance.

She could have used the photos to blackmail, but my guess was she hadn't. You blackmail and you get large bills. You earn it on your back and you get the small ones.

I felt dirty exploring her life. And dirty for what she did to get it.

Just plain dirty.

I looked around my fine office, my corner office, and felt secure. I had it lucky. But my luck had run out.

It was time — I had to look at the photos.

# Chapter 18

I PULLED THE WHITE envelope out of my jacket and dropped it in front of me.

It landed almost soundless.

I sat there and stared at it for a while, the white of the envelope cutting across the soft green of the blotter. A truck rumbled down on 7th below me. Other than that it was quiet. Just the hum of the fan to my left.

I pulled the pictures out and fanned them across my green blotter.

There were twelve of them in all. Snaps, really. In each one, there was a girl on a bed. The same bed, in the same room, and all the girls were gagged and tied.

And in each pic, on the other side of the bed from the camera, was a guy hitting them. But in three of them, I noticed a guy's leg along the right edge of the picture, the rest of him just out of view. The only thing visible was his pant leg and a shoe.

The pictures looked harsh and raw on my desk. I'd seen naked women before, and I'd seen people hitting people before. And yeah, men hitting women. I'd seen a lot of that. But here, caught in pictures in black and white… on purpose… lying there on my desk? I felt like I was a part of what was going on.

They were hard. Nasty.

Then I forced myself to look at them like a detective. Because I was.

They were obviously shot for blackmail. All the pics had a blurred and dark left edge, like the camera was set up in the same place every time, and it caught a little of whatever it was trying to hide it.

The shot just had the bed, and a white wall behind it and to the other side of it. To the right, along the top of each pic, was a small dark square cut off by the right edge. A small window, up high, by the looks of it. And along the top of the pics were dark boards running along where the ceiling should be. It was a raw, unfinished ceiling, and the dark boards above were floor joists from another floor above it. It was a basement. I'd been in enough of them to know.

Each of the pics had only one girl in them, and there were four different girls in all – Holly, and three others. Some of the girls were in a few of the pics, some in only one, but all of them were with a different guy. Except the tall bald guy. He was in five of Holly's pics.

I guess he had a favorite.

In most of the shots, you could see wisps of black hair from the back and sides, plastered across the top of his bald head with sweat he had worked up hitting her. Holly. In each of the pics, you could see the combination of hate and joy on his face. A sense of power.

I picked up one of them.

As hard as I could, I tried to think of the Holly I saw in the photo Rose gave me — young, beautiful — but all I could see was the harsh reality of what I held in my hand. A naked girl being hit. My breath shortened again and I could feel my entire body go tense. And my thoughts? My thoughts went to the tall bald guy, and to all the other guys hitting the girls in the other pictures. I felt the weight of my guns pulling down in their holsters, and

I wanted to use them on every one of them. Hit each of them. Worse than what they did to the girls.

I finally let out a breath that was choked up inside me. I had to stop. If I kept this up, I'd never get anywhere.

So I looked back down at Holly in the picture — as if she was just another clue.

And that was better. Almost.

I looked closer at the pic and could see there were a number of dark spots — black, really — running up and down her body. They were on her arms, chest, thighs, and yeah, even her face. Some were small, some were large, but the thing about bruises was — they were never dark to begin with. They needed time to get that way. Once a man hit a woman, the only thing left right away was a red mark. And the swelling.

I knew all about that.

After a day or two, that's when the hit would turn the shade of purple that always stayed for a while. Like the ones that looked black in the pictures. To remind you just what happened.

Holly was covered in them. The black ones. And there were some light ones in there, too. I pulled out all five snaps with Holly and the tall bald guy and laid them out in front of me. Then I pushed the other girls away so I could focus.

Five shots with Holly and the tall bald guy. In all of them, he wore different clothes. Five different days.

There wasn't much I could tell about him except the clothes he wore looked more expensive than the clothes the other guys wore. There were creases in his pants, they all looked almost new, and his shirts — they fit like they were made for him. There was a small monogram on the cuff of all his shirts but I couldn't make it out. His hand was too busy getting blurred as it shot down to hit Holly. Then I noticed something else.

In the photos, Holly's body was white, and the bruises were black. Most of them, anyway. But some were shades of gray, and I knew what that was. What they looked like in real life. The gray ones in the pictures were either just starting to form into the dark purple bruises, so were within one or two days of getting hit, or they were the yellow-green of a fading bruise, maybe a week, maybe two weeks old. So using when a mark first appeared, to when it turned black, to when it faded to soft gray, I could map out the order of when the pics were taken.

I arranged them in order and saw the story of Holly's life on that bed. With all the cash in the box and the fact that the photos were taken over a number of days, it meant she wasn't being held prisoner. She had decided to do it on her own. Decided to put herself through this.

The glass and bottle were still on my desk and I used them. Twice.

To get away from Holly, I pulled the other snaps down and arranged them on the blotter in front of me. Nothing stood out. Just a parade of naked girls in front of me, getting hit by a bunch of different guys.

Then I pulled out the three pictures with the leg on the right. It was pretty much in the same position in all three. In two of the shots the pants were dark, and in one of them they were light. But that's not what caught my attention.

I pulled a magnifying glass out of my top drawer and shifted one of my lamps over, then focused the glass down to the shoe that was visible under the pant leg. Checking all three shots, it looked like the shoe was the same. But the big thing was, the thickness of the sole.

It was thick.

Thick enough to make a short man feel just a little taller.

Carlo. Maybe Carlo. I wasn't sure. But I would find out. It's what Jim was paying me for.

And now — it's what I wanted.

# Chapter 19

THE NEXT MORNING I drove downtown on 7th, just passing Grand, the dark red brick and cream-colored trim of the Excelsior Hotel stretching up above me to my right.

It was actually cool out. The sky had a rare covering of cloud, but I knew at any moment that Southern California sky could cut through and torch us all. I'll be honest, the heat was a pain but that sun and sky were worth it to me.

Traffic was heavy and I ate the exhaust of a lot of cars and buses. A Red Car trolley with its deep red sides cut up the center of 7th and I wondered if maybe that wasn't the best way to travel. Leave the driving to someone else. But I liked the power to go where I wanted, when I wanted. So here I sat in traffic.

I had called Rose first thing to let her know about Holly. I gave it to her straight and let her know how she was found. I didn't tell her about the money or the snaps. Again, another thing I'd keep quiet until the time was right.

After the call to Rose, I stopped off to see Bartie.

He brought out the files so I could take a look at the names they had for the girls and look at the pictures of the bodies. Not the bodies, their faces.

I matched two of the four girls in Holly's pictures to Bartie's files: a Helen Humphries — and Holly.

The three other files Bartie had, matched the three other names that Carlo had on his list: Ruth Teesdon, Ellie Craft, and Dorthia Parks. The three other victims.

Ruth, Ellie, and Dorthia.

From Carlo's list, Ruth and Ellie worked at the Viceroy Hotel, where I was headed right now. Dorthia and Helen worked at the Santorini. And of course Holly, who wasn't on Carlo's list, worked for Rose at the Pacific Surf.

The first thing was to find out if there was anything going on with the victims — crazy boyfriends, odd customers, anything. That was the easiest. The next was to ask around and see if I could identify the two unknown girls in Holly's pics. They weren't in any of Bartie's five files, so I hoped they were still alive. If they were, they could connect me to the little room in the pics — and whoever ran it.

Judging from the shoes in the three pics, my money was on Carlo. And for the whole thing. But I wasn't going to leave anything out. I'd learned a long time ago that nothing was a sure bet.

I had two of the pics with me — one each of the two girls I couldn't identify yet. One was of a thin blonde who looked like a movie star. Or at least tried to. The other was of a more plain girl, a little more full in the face. She had dark curls on her head like the fashion five years ago.

The Pacific Surf and Viceroy were essentially downtown, while the Santorini was out near the ocean. If all the girls had been from one hotel, then it probably would have been a customer killing them. But with the Santorini so far away, it almost looked random. But the only thing all the girls had in common was their profession — and that they all worked for Jim, ultimately. And Carlo.

Maybe it was someone who had a beef against the System. Maybe it was the competition.

Who knew.

The only thing I did know was that I was headed for the Viceroy, and the person who ran it.

Mother Angela.

# Chapter 20

MOTHER ANGELA WAS NOT.

She was neither a mother nor an angel. Or maybe she was. I guess you could never tell about those things.

Mother Angela was small but stout as she greeted me in the kitchen at the back of the Viceroy. It was thick hot back in there with a black coal stove like we had back in Michigan. The smell of eggs and bacon and something else hung in the air.

Mother Angela may have been short, but she looked like she could heft a fifty pound bag of potatoes with one hand. Somewhere in her late fifties, her face was fleshy with wrinkles cut deep and the skin was rough like she put lye to it every night for cold cream.

Her hair was black, with gray streaks ravaging their way through it all, and was plastered straight down on her head, a few loose strands wisping out on the side like they wanted to be tamed.

And how best to describe her eyes... well, there were two of them. I'll start with that. The one on the left was squinted, while the one on the right was pushed open wider than was morally right. I guess trying to compensate for the other.

And they were blue. The brightest, lightest blue I'd ever seen.

All in all, she looked tired. Which I suppose is about right for a woman who cleaned and cooked and handled everything else for a hotel with twenty-odd whores.

She was a "maid" for the System.

"Hello." Her voice was soft, nothing like the way she looked. The smile on her face looked genuine, and there was a quality about her that just drew you in. Like you were safe with her.

All right, I take back everything I thought about her. Maybe she did fit the "mother" bill after all. "I'm John Devin. I'm not sure if Carlo mentioned I was coming, but I'm looking into… what's been happening to the girls."

"He did. And such a sad thing." She bent her head and made the sign of the cross, her black blouse opening a bit through an undone button. From inside, a small, golden cross glowed bright.

All right — I was really wrong about her. My manners suddenly snapped to. "Yes, ma'am."

I waited for her to stop her prayer, or whatever it was she was doing. I was a long-former Lutheran myself and didn't know much about Catholics. My mother was Lutheran and my father Catholic. She won that battle, mostly because he didn't practice anything but being a bastard.

Mother looked back up at me, her prayer finished. "Want some grub?"

I almost laughed. That was unexpected. "Sure."

According to Rose, maids did all the cooking, cleaning, and general upkeep of each hotel. Plus a few other things. It was more about keeping the girls happy. Well, if not happy, keep them there. If you're on your back all day, you had to eat at some point. The maids were also in charge of the money and the ledger — the book that had all the names and addresses of the clients, as well as how much money they took in each day.

Where the girls would make anywhere between eighteen to thirty dollars a week, maids brought in thirty to forty. It paid well, especially nowadays when a nickel would buy you a cup of coffee.

She grabbed a pot holder and opened the black door of the oven. From out of it, raw heat hit me like a slap. She pulled out a large cast iron skillet with—

"Baked eggs. My own recipe." Mother Angela closed the oven door and the harsh heat disappeared, leaving behind a smell of eggs and... I wasn't sure what else.

But it smelled amazing.

And I'd only had coffee for breakfast. "What is it?"

She set the black skillet on top of the oven. "Eggs, bacon, a little cheese. And a few other things."

It was the few other things I couldn't make out.

I stood up and looked into the skillet. It was amazing — a layer of gold eggs, browned just right on top. I could see small pieces of bacon in there, but it was still that other smell I wasn't sure of. "What's the few other things?"

She smiled. "Gotcha, didn't I?"

She did. And then she directed me to the small, thin-legged wood table against the wall with a red and white checked table cloth. I hadn't noticed it before, and it almost felt like home.

I sat down at the table, the fresh warmth of the oven filling the kitchen. She pulled a simple white plate from somewhere, put a large portion of egg on it, and set it down in front of me.

My mother could cook. But nothing against her, Mother Angela cooked better.

The cheese is what was browned on top and it was perfect. The eggs were fluffy, while the bacon gave everything a great salty taste, smoky almost. And then there was the other taste. It was an herb and I couldn't quite place it.

Mother Angela must have seen the question on my face. "Cumin."

"What?"

Mother smiled, her larger eye softening just a bit. "It's cumin. A Mexican spice. Well," she began, her voice dropped as if she were giving away the secret of the world. "It's from the Mediterranean, actually. But the Mexicans, they know how to use it."

I had never had, or thought of, or even dreamed of, something like this. The girls must love her. I think I was starting to.

I ate everything she had put on my plate, and she added more. Plus a cup of coffee that wasn't burned. It was good. As everything was. I wondered when I could come back for more questions.

I looked up at Mother, still standing in front of her stove, a peaceful look on her lined face as someone enjoyed what she had made. Holly's mother's face flashed into my mind. A face not unlike Mother's. Mother's was a little harder, but I wondered what they had both gone through in life.

I tried to remember my mother, but too much time had passed. I wondered if her face looked like theirs. I didn't think so, but it had been so long. I missed her. And I hadn't thought that in a while.

That made me think of the two pics I had in my coat pocket. I pulled them both out and laid them on the table in front of me. "You know either one of these girls?"

Mother Angela looked at them and didn't react a bit. Then she nodded toward the door. "Want a cigarette?"

"I don't smoke."

She looked at me like I was an odd man. I was.

I just never got a taste for them. Had my first one in France, threw up, and never looked at another one since. Somehow, I just didn't expect her to smoke.

But that's the way a lot of things had gone in the past ten years. Women were doing a lot of things you'd never expect.

Like smoking.

In the open.

# Chapter 21

I STEPPED DOWN THE three wooden steps out the back of the hotel that ended in a dirt patch at the back of the place. That patch reached out another ten feet to the dirt alley behind.

The temperature had warmed up from the time I had gotten there, but it was still cool after the heat of the kitchen.

An old black Model T sat parked against the falling wood fence separating the hotel from the property next door. On the other side of the back was a line of filthy black trash cans, all of them full, some with their lids knocked off, everything smelling powerfully bad, like rotting food. Which it probably mostly was. I didn't want to think what else was in there. At the back of a brothel.

Mother walked toward the Model T and pulled a partially smoked cigarette from the pocket of her skirt. It was rumpled and smoked about halfway down. Then she pulled a wooden match from the same pocket, struck it against the fender of the car, and lit the butt.

She looked like a monkey with a pencil.

Not like she looked like a monkey, but… I could just never get used to a woman with a cigarette. And looking at her, it felt like I was looking at something I shouldn't.

Mother looked up at me, a crooked smile on her face. "I learned it from the girls."

She took another puff, a little edge of awkwardness about it, as if it was something she hadn't done all her life. Hell, it couldn't have been. No women smoked. Usually. Well, not until the '20s.

She reached out to me. "Lemme see those again."

I gave her the two pics again and she studied them in her free hand, shuffling them back and forth with the one that held the cigarette. The finger that held the cigarette was odd, curled over it like a hawk holding down prey.

Finally she handed the pics back. "I ain't seen either one of them. They're not any of my girls, and they haven't come through here."

She didn't seem to even react to what was going on in the pictures. "Have you ever heard of men doing this?"

Mother Angela laughed. "Hell, they do it all the time."

I knew that. All too well. "I didn't mean it that way."

She looked at me. "I know you didn't."

"You ever hear about anyone setting something like this up?"

"You mean for the blackmail?"

She was fast. "That, but also — have you ever heard of another hotel setting something like this up? The hitting?"

She looked at me close. "You mean another System hotel?"

"Yeah."

"No." She kept looking at the photos, first the one of the blonde trying to be a movie star, then the plain one with the dark curls. "And I don't recognize the room." She handed me back the pics. "You were going to ask me that, too, right?"

She really was fast. "Yeah."

"Sorry. Not doing you much good."

"So you knew Ruth and Ellie."

"Ruthie. Ruthie and Ellie, yes. It was a shame for those two."

"What about Ellie — any boyfriends, any customers acting a little strange?"

"No."

"And Ruthie?"

She sighed. "Sorry, none there either." She took another puff from her cigarette.

A small breeze drifted the smell of the garbage over to us. Mother didn't seem to notice. "Why do they get started?" It was a question I never asked Rose. Hell, I never even thought about it. Before.

"The girls?"

I nodded.

Mother looked off into the alley, onto the dry, hard dirt lying out there. The LA sun was out now and starting to beat down on it.

Nothing moved. Mother's voice went softer as she sat down on the fender of the Model T. "Money. You need money, and when you can't make one thing work, you try another. People don't want you. Think you ain't worth nothing," she looked up at me, "so you end up here. Ain't no harm in that, you're just trying to survive. You have dreams of something else, but then that gets taken away from you and you end up back here."

Mother Angela brought her cigarette up and pulled in, then breathed out smoke as if it were falling out of her like water from a fall. Everything was strangely still.

The cigarette burned down close to her fingertips. She didn't react. Maybe she couldn't feel it. Maybe she did, and it didn't matter.

Then she just dropped the burned-down cigarette to the hard ground. She pressed her hard black shoe into it, scuffed and scraped at it, and slowly, methodically, ground the cigarette down until it was just a charred, white-ended broken stick, lying in the dirt.

"Any girls around today who knew them?"

"Yeah. Not that there's a lot around today. They're not coming to work lately. All scared." Mother Angela laughed at this, hard and dry. Then coughed. "Millie's here. She knew 'em both. You talk to her if you want to know."

Then Mother pushed her stout body up off the bumper.

I reached out a hand to help her but she waved it off, then

walked back inside.

Time for me to find out if any of them knew Carlo. Personally. It was time to get some answers.

# Chapter 22

I SHOWED UP TO room fourteen and knocked.

"It's open."

I opened the door into a small room, about twelve by twelve, with a single window opposite the door, a single oak chair to the right, and a single bed to the left. The bed had white sheets over it, and a girl on top of those. "Millie?"

She looked up at me, confusion on her face. She wore red lipstick, and had white, bottle-blonde hair curled loose against her head like a movie star. Her cheeks were soft. Her eyes were sharp. And brown. And her body drifted down from there, thin and small, and not all that bad to look at.

She was dressed only in a white slip.

And there must have been a cool breeze in the room.

Judging by the slip.

Millie looked over at a small brass alarm clock sitting on the windowsill. "You're early. But I guess that's okay." Her voice was low-pitched for her size, I guess you could say sultry. Maybe her hair was originally brown. It would have matched her voice better.

"Actually I'm not... who you were expecting. Mother Angela sent me up. I'm a PI, looking into some things."

Millie immediately went silent, but looked at me with those sharp brown eyes. Sizing me up, I guess.

Then she reached under the bed and pulled out a packet of cigarettes and an ashtray. Again, a woman with cigarettes. She pulled out a man's steel lighter and lit the cigarette, then put it between her lips. Then she smiled, sultry. "You sure you don't want to be a customer?" Her eyes bit into me even more. "Something says we'd be fun."

She sat back against the dark wood headboard of the bed. One I'm sure that had seen a lot in its lifetime here at the hotel. "Sorry, no fun today. Someone's paying me to get a little information."

She smiled a very, very not-shy smile. I think she was enjoying this. "What do you get paid for getting information?"

"Enough."

"Expenses?"

"Yeah."

"Then think of me as an expense." Then she dropped one thin strap from her slip and it fell down low on her arm. The top curve of a breast laid out like fruit before a feast.

I cleared my throat. An old trick I used to get myself back on track. I hadn't needed it in a while. "Ruthie, we're going to talk about Ruthie. And Ellie."

"Oh…" Millie looked genuinely disappointed. She put the cigarette back in her mouth and this time got busy with it. The tip of it glowed a bright orange, then dropped back down to a dirty red. Then she exhaled, the smoke blowing out full-front as if she were trying to put up a screen.

I didn't trust myself near the bed, so I walked over and planted myself on the chair. It was uncomfortable. Good. "What can you tell me about them?"

"That's a stupid question."

"Why?"

"Because I don't have all day. And obviously you don't have all day, otherwise you would be over here discussing how to spend that expense money. You sure you don't want a little fun?"

"I'm sure."

"You're not fun."

"I've been told that."

"By women?"

"By a lot of people. So, who killed them?"

Millie smiled. "See there, right to the point. Now I'm beginning to like you."

I was, too. Her. "You didn't before?" I liked a strong dame.

"I liked your expense money. But…" She took another puff of her cigarette, then flicked the ashes down onto the floor. "I'm off later this afternoon. Want to swing around to my place? Gratis?"

"Gratis is a big word."

"Oh, I've learned a lot of things. Want me to show you?"

This girl had a one-track mind. I suppose it helped in her line of work. "You all do that? Invite customers home?"

Millie looked at me. "It depends on what you're reporting back to whoever hired you. And just who did hire you?"

"People who don't like their employees killed."

"Oh. In that case, we never invite customers home. That would be cheating." She smiled.

"Don't worry. I pay for my information and you don't have to do a thing."

"What if I want to do a thing? And more things after that?" She smiled even more. And there seemed like there was a hint of lioness around the edges of it. The real meat-eating kind.

"Find someone else. But — that brings up an interesting point. How many girls took home work?"

Millie seemed to tire of me. She finished her cigarette and stubbed it out into the four-cornered glass ashtray. When she leaned down to get it her slip slipped open, not leaving anything to the imagination.

She came back up from below the bed and… caught me looking. She smiled. And left her legs spread apart a bit. With me down at the end of the bed.

I tried to keep my eyes on her eyes.

She pulled a tube of lipstick out from under her pillow and fixed her lips. "You sure?"

This was not what I expected. "Actually, I'm not. But it isn't going to happen, sister. Strictly work."

"Me, too." She smiled. "Well, not work. Fun." The smile dropped from her lips and she looked at me. "Maybe I work like this, but I'm also a girl. A regular girl. And sometimes I like to be one."

I pulled out a ten, walked over to her and dropped it on the bed next to her. Well away from anything funny. Then I walked to the far corner of the room and leaned into it. As far away from her as I could get. "Now, tell me about Ruthie and Ellie."

Then she smiled again and laughed. "I like you. But what's it going to take to wear you down?"

I wondered myself.

I was in the Marines in France, Belgium, and Germany during the Great War, and fighting in Shanghai, China after it. I had never faced a more difficult assault than Miss Millie.

And it kept coming.

# Chapter 23

I'D QUESTIONED MILLIE FOR a while about Ellie and there was nothing there. Except that she hated her. Definitely oil and water, and no, she didn't kill her.

Talking didn't seem to be something she liked. Or rather, getting down to what I really wanted didn't seem too appealing to her. "What about Ruthie?"

"She was a girl, what can I say?"

Millie sat on the bed. At least her mouth was keeping busy with the cigarette, because it sure wasn't working too hard to give me information. She looked absently out the window, not at much of anything, because there wasn't anything there. Just 2nd outside it, and a couple of one-story supply buildings on the other side.

The window was open, trying to let in a breeze if there was one, but there wasn't. The only thing it let in were traffic noises. Cars mostly, with heavy trucks passing every once in a while. The usual. It was Los Angeles.

"She have any boyfriends?"

No answer.

"She take any clients home with her ever?"

Millie was starting to get mad, I could see it in her. Or maybe it was something else. Shut down.

She took another puff from her cigarette. Still no answer.

"Did you kill her?"

No answer.

Then Millie looked over at me. I couldn't make out what was in her brown eyes. They were flat. Then her cigarette finally separated from her mouth. "What do you care?"

"I don't care, I'm just trying to take care of this mess. See if I can catch the killer so you all don't have to worry anymore."

She eyed me from her bed. She was comfortable there. It was hers. She owned it. And she didn't have to say a damn thing if she didn't want to.

A queen, in a satin slip wanting to be silk, on a bed wanting to be a throne. Smoke still rose from her cigarette, dissipating into the smoke-choked air above her, everything held in close by walls on all four sides. "Get out."

"Listen, Millie, I—"

"You remembered my name. How's that? How'd you manage to do that, Mr. PI? Mr. 'Hand me a sawbuck' because I ain't really nothin' to you. Am I right?"

"Look, Millie…"

"Am I right??" She was getting a little unhinged.

All I wanted to do was ask some questions, and I get this. "Did you actually know Ruthie?"

"Everyone knew Ruthie." Millie got up off the bed, impatient with all the questions. She walked over to the window in her slip and stood there, looking out.

I guess as a prostitute you get used to being naked, used to being… in front of people. But standing in front of the open window, still somehow kind of threw me off. I've seen a lot in my life, including whores and killing and all the worst that men can do, but I guess there's still a little bit of the Midwest farmboy in me. A woman, standing practically naked in front of a window, just somehow was… different for me.

"What do you remember most about her?" It's a question I

used sometimes.

It wasn't direct, but sometimes it got people talking. Especially the ones who didn't want to.

Millie didn't say anything at first, the curl of smoke drifting up between her and the window until it met with the cloud of it above her. Then she sat down on the floor, her head just making it up to the windowsill as she looked out. Her legs were curled back under her and I couldn't stop thinking how she looked like a young girl sitting there, watching the world go by below. "She always smiled."

"Yeah?"

"Yeah. More than the rest of us, but none of us smiled, so I guess... she would smile more than the rest of us, huh?"

"Was she happy?"

Millie looked back around, her face dark with the light of the window coming in back of her. A lot seemed to cross her face as she sat there. Then she took a puff of her cigarette, then turned back around looking out. "Are you happy?"

Interesting question. "I never thought about it. I'm too busy trying to keep a roof over a few people's heads."

"You married?"

"No."

"Then who you keeping the roofs for?"

"My secretary. Me. A kid I know. Separate roofs."

"A real white knight, huh?"

Not even close. "Just trying to do at least a couple things right in my life."

Then Millie turned her entire body around, her legs straight out on the floor in front of her, leaning her back against the bare wall below the window. She looked small there as she looked up at me, her hands in her lap, smoke from the cigarette still curling up. "I guess that makes a few of us."

"Give me anything you can on Ruthie. I'm just trying to figure out who did it."

"Do you care?"

I thought about the picture of Holly's mother against the barn. I thought about the picture of Holly that Rose had given me. Not the others. "Yeah, I do."

"There's been a few, right?"

"The killings? Yeah. Five."

"Who else?"

I told her all five, but when I got to Holly's name Millie's head snapped up, then it went back down. Fast.

"What? You know Holly?"

She nodded. But she held something hard inside.

"What's wrong?"

She was locked up. Silent again. She knew something about Holly.

Millie tossed her head and tried to throw off the shock. "We all know each other. At least... we get around." She looked out the window to get away from my eyes. "If they don't need us at one hotel, sometimes we'll work at another. Or sometimes we start at one hotel, then move to another."

"And that's how you met Holly?"

The traffic outside was uncharacteristically dead.

It was bone-silent in the room.

Millie pulled out another cigarette and lit it. The paper and tobacco crackled lightly as she pulled at it.

Then she blew it out. "Yeah."

She was closed up hard on Holly and I knew I wasn't going to get any more from her, at least for now. So I hit her from the side. "What about Carlo?"

Her eyes snapped back to me like she had actually been hit. "What about Carlo?"

"You ever hear about him taking any of you to a place where women were... hit on purpose?"

She laughed, a thin laugh that didn't suit her. "They're all on purpose."

I'd seen enough of Millie's body there in the room to know she didn't have any bruises. At least the ones that showed.

She looked up at me, I don't know, maybe searching for something, then shot her eyes down to the floor in front of her. Maybe trying to get away from the question.

Then she opened up. "Yeah, kind of."

"Kind of meaning you, or other girls."

"Me, and two others."

Maybe we were getting somewhere. "Any of the girls I mentioned?"

"No."

"How long ago was this?"

"Two years."

Too long ago for what had been happening recently. Unless there were others dead.

"It was a party. For a full weekend." She took another drag on her cigarette and blew it out soft, like she was lost in it. "One hundred dollars I got, which ain't no small change."

"What happened?"

"Carlo stopped by the hotel and asked me if I was interested in a party. With some millionaires on a yacht." She looked around the room. "I figured it had to be better than this place."

"Where was it?"

"Long Beach. It was parked down there, and when me and the other girls got there, it started out all fun. They took us out and talked about maybe going to Catalina. The waves weren't bad and that was the part I was worried about. Then on the second night after we had all gotten a little loopy, one of the guys hit me. Just right out of the blue. He was the one who owned the yacht."

"Were any of the other girls hit?"

"No. Just me." She got up from the bed and walked back over to the window. I think she liked the light there. "We were horsing around on the bed, in the main cabin, and he just hauled off on me. Hit me right in the thigh."

Tension shot through me. "What'd he look like?"

She looked back at me. "Tall. He was tall. In his forties, maybe."

"What kind of hair?"

She looked at me funny. "Not much of it. He was bald, except for some black hair around the sides and back. But not much. Why?"

The guy in the snaps with Holly. I tried to hold in everything that wanted to come out. "Nothing. Go on."

She turned back to the window. "It caught both of us by surprise. I didn't expect it and the way he looked, he looked like he surprised himself. Then he real quick got this look in his face, like he liked it. He smiled. Then he slugged me again. Then he got out of the bed all happy and pulled out a fin from his wallet and set it on the bed next to me. Then he hit me some more. I told him not to, but he kept laying down more money."

Millie stood there, her back still to me, the light from the window silhouetting her naked form beneath her slip. She wasn't crying.

"I didn't want the money. I just wanted him to stop."

I wanted to walk over to her, but something — everything — was confusing about all this. I wasn't sure what to do. "What happened?"

She shrugged. "The weekend ended." She turned around and took a puff of her cigarette as if nothing had happened, but I could see the small shake in her hand as she pulled the cigarette back away from her lips. Then she sat back down on the floor under the window and ground out the cigarette on the floor. "It took me two weeks to recover. Then I went to Carlo and almost ripped his head off."

"What happened?"

Milie laughed. "Nothing. He asked me if I liked it. And he was serious. I told him what he could do with himself, but all he did was laugh. Then he gave me an extra hundred."

Holly's pics didn't look like they were on a yacht. It was too plain. "Any of the other girls talk about being invited onto the yacht?"

"No. But Carlo stopped by another time, about a month after, and asked me if I wanted to come to a party. I asked him if it was on a yacht and he laughed and said no. Then he smiled, said that particular customer really liked me, and he was starting what he was calling 'black-and-blue parties.' Said it would pay double. Then I told him to stuff himself, and if he ever came at me with anything like that again, I'd mention it to Mother Angela and let her talk to him. He didn't like that any, and really, he looked like he was going to smack me. But then Vince quieted him down."

"Vince was with him?"

Millie laughed. "Vince is always with him. Then Carlo pulled two hundreds out of his pocket and held them in front of me. He told me to keep my mouth shut, and he'd never invite me for another party again."

"Did you ever hear of any other of those black-and-blue parties?"

She didn't look at me. Then her eyes dropped down and she crushed her cigarette out on the floor, grinding it in for about as far as it would go. It was a smashed bit of white paper and black ash. "I've never been treated so bad in my life. Like I was trash."

I didn't like Carlo before, but I was starting to feel a few other things toward him. "I got no standing, telling anyone how they should make their money. But seems to me, somebody does that to someone, they shouldn't be allowed to continue. The guy on the yacht, or Carlo."

Millie picked a speck of tobacco from her tongue. She looked at the speck on her finger, then up at me, then flicked the speck to somewhere in the corner of the room. Far, far away.

She looked at me like she wanted to say more, a lot more.

But she didn't. Then finally she did.

"If a girl was going to buy you a drink, where would she do it?"

That was unexpected.

A lot raced around inside me, including how bad it was to get mixed up with anyone even remotely tied to a case. But I knew she knew more about Holly. But then my thoughts went to who she was, what she did.

It was confusing. What was going on inside my head, and what was going on in parts south of there.

She was part of a case and she… worked for a living. That wasn't something I'd ever thought about. But then what did I just say — I got no standing telling someone how to make their money. I made mine investigating. That's lower than a cop. I always made it about trying to help someone. That's how I justified it in my head, and to be honest, it's what made it feel like I was doing something with my life. A lot of something sometimes. But a lot of people didn't think much of me. So who was I to judge someone for what they did?

I looked at her. She was just a girl, sitting on the floor in front of a window, opened out to the rest of a city that was full of a lot of things wrong.

She cocked her head and shrugged her shoulders. "I ain't looking for a ring, Mr. PI. Just a drink."

What the hell, I liked her eyes. "You know Toots'?"

"Over by—"

"Yeah."

She smiled. "I know it."

"I do, too. And sometimes I even go there."

That wasn't how it was all supposed to be happening. At least not the way I was raised. A girl was sitting in front of me, half naked, smoking, and she had — asked me out. I think on a date. And she was… what she was.

This didn't fit into any way that I was raised. Although I wasn't exactly raised to kill a man at sixteen, but I did anyway. In the war.

The whole world was crashing around me — the stock market, money… women. And I had no idea what the new rules were. All bets were off it seemed nowadays. Nothing was the same. Nothing was what you were expecting.

Of course what had I learned since I became a PI? That nothing, was ever the way I expected.

Then through all of this I realized I had a bit of a smile planted on my face. I quickly ripped it off and took control. "Eight?"

She smiled. "Eight."

This was going to be interesting. I think I forgot how to talk to women, at least when a case wasn't involved. The most I talked to women these days was to Bella. About cases, paying bills, and whether or not I'd cracked the Washington safe yet. But this?

Was a whole other ball of wax.

So I got out of her room. Fast.

Before she talked me into something else.

# Chapter 24

BEFORE I LEFT, I checked with some of the other girls at the Viceroy, at least the ones who were there.

Ruthie was the top earner at the hotel, while Ellie complained a lot and the girls didn't like her. Ruthie was from Chicago and hated the snow, Ellie was from Mississippi and hated the humidity. Other than that, there was no mention of any boyfriends, or any customers that seemed out of place. Or out of their mind.

I also showed Holly's two pictures of the girls I couldn't place yet, and none of the girls at the Viceroy could either. One of the girls thought the plain-looking one with the dark curls was vaguely familiar, but she wasn't sure if it was because she'd seen her at one of the hotels, or at some shop downtown. Or even if she'd seen her at all.

None of them knew Carlo at all. And when I asked them about what was happening on the bed with Holly and the other girls in the pics, they shut up. I think it had more to do with them thanking God they weren't on those beds themselves. But either way, they hadn't heard of anything like that happening with any of the hotels they'd worked out of. And yeah, that included the Santorini.

I checked back in with Mother Angela and she, of course, knew Carlo. She got quiet when I pushed for more and pretty much shut me up in the end, saying she just tried to stay out of his way.

As for the hitting, she hadn't heard anything about that.

But she did look a lot on the disgusted side as she looked at the pics. Like she wanted to get whoever set it all up — and the guys doing the hitting.

My next stop I didn't want to do, but there you have it. You always gotta do what you don't want. Mostly because nobody else is going to do it for you.

Especially when it involved pain.

# Chapter 25

THE PAIN WASN'T MINE, it was going to be Rose's. When I asked her more about Holly.

I pulled up in front of her hotel around noon, the sun beating down.

The hotel was the Pacific Surf, just off 2nd downtown. A gray, three story thing with a flat roof and trim around the windows the color of red brick. The sign out front was plain black letters on white wood.

It all looked slap-dash, like it wasn't really a hotel. And of course it wasn't, except for the few tenants they kept to make the place look legitimate.

Rose sat in a small office at the back of the place, the last door on the left of the main hall leading down the center of the building. There was no automatic elevator.

Inside was a simple table set up against the far wall, with an older, wood, swivel chair in front of it. Rose sat in the chair and it tilted a bit to the left. "So this is your place…"

Rose started, then swiveled around to see me, her simple gray housedress a lot different from the flowing red dress I usually saw her in. "Devin…"

A shadow fell over her face. Her eyes darted around the small office and I wondered if maybe she was embarrassed. A small tan filing cabinet, four drawer, was tucked in the corner to her right. The walls were a dark green, and a small window next to Rose looked out onto the side of the building next door, about three feet away. Red brick, that's all I could see.

There was no rug over the bare wood planks that made up the floor. They were scuffed and scarred from a lot of years of use. Heavy dust sat along the edges where the green walls met the floor, and there was a dry smell to the place. All in all, it felt small and dim. Not a great place to spend your life, but, at least it was a job.

Rose's mouth angled crookedly. "I don't have another chair." Then she mumbled almost. "That's why I always say the Angel."

She was embarrassed, that's why she always wanted to meet at the diner. I softened my mug into an almost smile. "I figured this would be a little more private."

"Hmm…" She spun her chair around to face the desk and put away a small book. The hotel's ledger, most likely. "I suppose."

I walked in and shut the door softly behind me, then leaned back against it. "I'm sorry about the call this morning, Rose. About Holly."

"Yeah." She still faced forward, and didn't say anything more.

Rose was never the type to be too emotional, at least all the times I'd talked with her, and some of those were just sharing a breakfast for no reason. But still, she's the one asked me to look for Holly. She had to be hurting. "I found a few things. Not a lot but, it's something." I pulled out the pics of the two girls I didn't know yet. I wasn't about to show her Holly. I didn't think Rose would hold up too well seeing her that way.

But in the two pics, the girls were plenty bruised. "You know either of these girls?"

Rose turned around and held out her wrinkled hand, draped with a large gold ring with a red stone on it, and took the pics. Her reaction wasn't good. "Where the hell'd you get these?" Her eyes didn't leave the pictures, shuffling between them, looking at the guys hitting naked girls.

They still looked dirty. Even when someone else held them. "Let's just say I found 'em. Do you know either of them?"

"This one," she pointed at the picture of the blonde trying to look like a movie star, "That's Anna. Banko." Rose's shoulders had slumped. I heard a muffled, but distinctive thumping coming from above. "She… she left town maybe three, four months ago."

"Left, or you haven't seen her?" I wondered if there was a sixth girl lying dead somewhere.

"Left." Rose looked up at me. "She stopped here on the way out of town. Said she was moving on. She started here before she moved on to the Santorini."

Another one at the Santorini. "She have any bruises?"

Rose looked back at the photo and mumbled, "No. Not that I saw." She looked back up at me. "Where did you get these?"

"I really can't tell you, Rose. Not right now." I nodded back toward the photo in her hand. "That kind of thing go on at the hotels?"

Rose's jaw adjusted back and forth. Like she was stretching it to get out some kind of tension that had sat there for too long. "Ropes? Sometimes." Her voice dropped to a whisper. "But not the…" She took in another great, slow, gasp of air, but didn't let it out.

And she didn't.

And then she did.

It came in shuddering escapes, her jaw working slow back and forth. "I don't put up with the other."

I felt bad… for all of them. "What about the other hotels? Does the System allow—"

"It ain't about allowing. We stop it. Me, Mother, I don't think any of us allow that. Because guys who want that? They're a problem. Always a problem, so you don't let it in the door in the first place. You never let them come back."

Rose's eyes didn't leave the photo; then she touched it, along the lower edge. Maybe she wanted to touch the girl, but she couldn't bring herself to do it.

"You recognize the room?"

Rose looked up, directly at me. She shook her head, but I could see in her eyes that she wanted to know. Wanted to recognize it. Wanted to help. But she couldn't.

I pulled out one of the other photos, one with Helen in it — and a man's leg along the right side with a shoe visible. "I think that's Carlo. I'm not sure, but…"

Rose took that one and studied it. "He do it?" Her eyes went to razors. I could see the rage bottled up inside her.

"I'm not sure. That's what I'm trying to find out."

Rose's wide hips adjusted on the chair and the tilted thing squealed at the movement.

"Have you ever heard about something called a black-and-blue party?"

Rose's eyes got hard, and dark. "You telling me he and that little friend of his set up something like this?"

"I'm not sure yet. But that's what I'm thinking."

"You get him."

"Rose, listen. Jim asked me to look into this, and that's what I'm doing. I'll find out. And just so you know, I didn't tell him about you asking about Holly."

"Why?"

"I just wanted to keep you out of—"

"I meant why's Jim interested?"

I shrugged my shoulders. "He says the girls are starting to get scared. They're refusing to come in."

Rose nodded. "That's a fact." She pointed to the three pictures in her hand. "You think Carlo and Vince killed all those girls? Killed Holly?"

"Like I say, I don't know. But if he did, they did, the only thing that doesn't add up is, why dump the… bodies where they'll be found? That doesn't make any sense."

A sarcastic smile cut across her face. "And cutting up girls makes sense?"

"No, it's…" But that was a good point. Anyone crazy enough to cut someone up that way was crazy enough to drop off the bodies. People usually dumped bodies out in the mountains. Let the animals take care of them. "I was just thinking, a person who doesn't want to get caught hides the bodies. Buries them. And here — they're cutting them up and leaving them out where people can find them. So who cuts up…" Then I stopped.

A tear sat at the corner of Rose's eye. A big one. It stayed there, longer than any tear had a right to, almost defying the simple laws of nature.

Then it dropped. Hard and fast and fell off the plump part of her cheek to land on the front of her dress. The gray fabric darkened to a wet blackness where it landed.

"I'm sorry, Rose."

"You'll get him, right?"

"I'll get him." That I knew for sure.

"Thanks. And thanks for not mentioning me to Jim."

I nodded.

I still had one more girl to find — the plain one with the dark curls. And a room. A room where everything happened.

If I could find the room, I could stop it.

All of it.

# Chapter 26

I STOPPED TO SEE a guy I knew in the LA County Assessor's Office. After a quick check, he found three properties owned by Carlo, and none for Vince. Apparently Carlo wasn't paying him enough.

By the time I'd gotten to the Assessor's Office, and to the first two properties, it was already afternoon. Which was actually pretty good in the end because I got to see kids playing outside the first address, a small house on the east side of Venice. Didn't much look like any place Carlo and Vince would cut up women. Then, when a woman came out of the house to call the kids inside, I was sure of it.

Looked like Carlo was actually smart. He owned property that he rented out. Go figure.

The second piece of property was a small diner at Olympic and Vermont. Nothing special, with everything out front except a small kitchen in the back. If there was any place to cut up women, it wasn't here where I was looking. So I ordered a cup of coffee and talked with the waitress a bit. Sometimes the best questions are the ones you ask out of the blue. It knocks people back on their heels, and usually they'll either answer or call you an idiot.

I asked her, and she answered, and she didn't call me an idiot. There was no basement.

Strike number two on the property front.

The third address was a warehouse on 11th downtown.

I pulled up and there wasn't much traffic around. It looked like all the other warehouses in the area were either closed or abandoned. I suppose when the economy goes to hell as fast as this one was doing, there wasn't much need to store things. Because nobody can afford to buy anything in the first place.

I parked a little ways down from the warehouse and watched for a few minutes.

Nobody was coming or going.

I got out and crossed the street and walked up slow to the place. It was old and ramshackle. A one story all flat thing, it was all red brick, flat roof, and seemed to lean a bit to the left.

There was one regular wood door with no windows heading into the place, a small four-paned window next to that, and a big rolling door on the face of the building, like what we used to have on the front of the barn back home. The rolling door was chained and padlocked. The new lock didn't bother me any. I could get into it easy, but shoving that door aside after I got it open was not my idea of fun. So I went to the regular door.

A quick check in the window to the side, after I brushed a load of grime off it, showed a small reception area with a counter. Yellowing scraps of paper littered the counter along with what looked like a healthy layer of dust. A doorway behind the counter led to the back. It looked like nobody'd been in the place for years.

My breathing sped up.

I looked back over my shoulder. The road and warehouse across the street were quiet, nobody still around, so I pulled out my picks and got to work.

I was inside fast and swept the door closed behind me, then just as quick pulled both my guns.

I liked the heavy feel of them in my hands. They'd make for nice hammers to beat the hell out of whoever I found inside. If

I found anybody.

But I listened for a bit and there was nothing. The smell of oil, grease, and dust lay still in the air, like it had been a long time since any of it had been disturbed. I headed for the doorway behind the counter.

Down the narrow hall, there were two offices that sat to either side. Each was small and looked like the other, and was definitely not big enough for a bed. Nothing was disturbed and nothing looked interesting in either, so I headed for the gray metal door at the far end.

I listened at it, but nothing came from the other side. The only thing was the hair on the back of my head started to stand up. Like it wasn't sure, but it thought there was somebody in the place.

I holstered one gun and put my hand on the cold brass knob of the door, and opened it slow.

I slipped into the large open space of the main part of the warehouse.

It actually didn't look like a warehouse, more like a repair place for trucks and heavy equipment. There was a large open space to my right where the trucks were driven into the place, then in front of me stretched rows of long wooden shelving units that ran ten feet into the air.

Oil looked, and smelled, like it was soaked into everything. But other than the shelves, mostly empty, there didn't look to be anything else in the place.

I pulled my other gun and walked back through the shelves. There was the occasional cardboard box, dry and drooping with age, some with markings on them of what they used to hold — belts, alternators, oil. Lots of boxes that said they had oil. But other than that, it was just a forest of shelves.

Looking up and down the rows, I had the sense that at one time the place must have been busy, but judging by the thick layer of dust on everything, that had to have been a few years ago. Now the place sat without anyone in it. I wasn't sure whether that was because Carlo was using it to host black-and-blue parties, or because after the crash he couldn't rent the place. My guess was the second.

I got back to the back wall of the place and there was nothing. Walking the length of the back row, I only saw the wall to the place, with no extra doors. The floor looked solid and there were no trap doors down into some secret chamber.

There were no mattresses sitting on a shelf. No rope used for tying. Nothing.

It just didn't feel right.

The room had to be in the basement of a house.

I holstered my guns, feeling a little bad I wasn't able to use them on anyone.

As I stood there, the quiet and the smell of oil and grease gathered around me.

I had Carlo. At least I thought I had him. Well, what I really had was five dead girls, all cut up, some with bad bruises and some without any. They all worked for Jim, from three separate hotels. And Holly's pictures.

And no bed. Yet.

I needed to find that third girl in Holly's pictures. And I needed to find where the bed was. Still.

I looked at my watch and it was already nearing six. Then something hit me. Maybe it was fear, I don't know. I'd been in trenches, shot at, had shells shot at me, and I'd killed enough men in hand-to-hand combat to fill some of those trenches — but at eight, I had to meet Millie at Toots'.

And that had me… concerned.

Well, it was part of the case. She knew something about Holly, and if I pressed her hard enough, she may even tell me about it. And anything else she knew about Carlo. She had to know something else.

It was time to go, so I headed for the door back to the front. Being a thorough guy, I decided to check the offices one more time in case I missed something, and as I turned into the first, a fist caught me full-on in the face. Like a truck.

I fell backward and into the office across the hall and hit the floor, my elbow smacking into the concrete floor below me. I reached for a gun with the other hand, but a huge guy in a dark suit and black fedora came at me through the door and crashed his huge foot into the gun, launching it, clattering to the floor in back of me.

It all happened too fast, but not so fast that I couldn't shoot my own foot up to catch him between the legs. The big guy doubled over, his face coming right toward me, so I brought up a fist and caught him square in the side of the head and he dropped like a felled oak. I guess I caught his temple.

He slammed into the floor face-first to the side of me, the sound a nice thick thud, like a wet melon hitting dirt.

I scrambled over the top of him, grabbed his shoulder, and yanked him over to face me. His black hat fell off — and he had a full head of hair. Not the tall bald guy at all.

This guy was big, and wide, and his face was younger and more full. Like he hadn't lost his baby fat yet. I placed him maybe in his early thirties, and if he was standing, he was probably a good six foot six. A monster.

Maybe it was the guy who came after Eula.

I reached toward his jacket to look for a wallet. Unfortunately, without even cracking an eye, the guy's fist shot up and caught me back in the head.

I fell to the side and before I knew it, the big guy wrestled me into a bear hug, both of us sitting on the floor, him behind me. The thing was, he held me around the body with only one arm, pinning both of mine. Then he had his other arm wrapped around my throat.

He spoke right into my ear, his hot breath feeling unnatural against me. "Stop lookin' into things where you don't belong."

His chokehold was strangling but I could tell he wasn't looking to kill me, on account of I could still actually breathe. Which meant I could croak out a few words. "I just wondered if this place was for sale. You own it?"

The big guy let off the choke-hold a little and smacked me in the head, like you'd smack a little brother. "Don't be funnin' me." Then he clamped right back down on my throat.

As he held me, I tried to shift so I could get one of my guns; but he clamped down even harder over my arms. "Don't ask no more questions about the girls, all right?"

"What girls?"

He smacked me in the head again. Twice. "I said don't fun me!"

Then he hit me even harder. That rung me, and I felt a little light-headed. Of course, that could also be because of the oxygen being choked out of me.

"Leave the girls alone. Stop it."

"Who are you—"

But that's the last thing I said, because something crashed into my head like a meteor.

And I was out.

# Chapter 27

FINALLY, THE HAPPIEST MOMENT of the day.

It was night and I sat with a drink in front of me at Toots' — which was a *far* sight better than waking up with a split head in a warehouse. I'd find that big guy and return it. Soon, I hoped.

Toots is both a guy, and a speakeasy. The guy is a huge Mick from County Wexford, and the speakeasy, Toots', is located in the back of a deli. Well, the deli is really just the fake front. Nothing is ever what you think in LA.

"Have some more. You look like you need it," Toots said, standing six-foot-five in front of me. His sandy red hair was in a short pompadour, his full pink face giving me the generous smile that was always there — unless you crossed him. Then you were going to die.

Toots tipped another couple of fingers of Jameson into my glass, direct from the only bottle of it in the place — that belonged to me, and would never run out.

I did him a favor once.

And Toots has a long memory.

I looked up at Toots, offered a toast, then took a small sip of the stuff. It burned my split lip on the way in, but since I was already in the sipping phase of the evening, the whisky had already taken care of all the other hurts that came from the beating.

I had woken up in the warehouse at seven, still bleeding. I had just enough time to get to Toots', stop the bloody nose, clean up most of my face, and sit down at my favorite spot at the end of the fifty-foot bar. Near my bottle.

Toots smiled, even bigger. "You still look like hell."

"Thanks."

"Don't mention it." He put away the bottle on the top shelf, took one more look back at me, shook his head, then headed up the bar.

He was a good guy. Family for me here in a place I had none.

The place wasn't too crowded but to my right, around the corner from me at the bar, was Ada. She was old, and small, with long gray hair pulled back into a tight bun at the back of her head. Her dark brown hickory cane sat on the bar next to her and she had her usual — one beer — sitting in front of her. The beer was almost gone but the woman was anything but. Feisty, that's what my mother would have called her. At least when she wanted to be. But a lot of the time she was content to sit at the bar watching everything else go by, with her eyes missing none of it. "Walk into a door?"

It was the first thing she'd said to me, and I'd been sitting there with my drink for almost half an hour. She was a pill. "More like an elephant."

"How'd the elephant make out?"

"Pretty good. This time, anyway." I smiled a wicked grin, and she returned it.

Then I spotted Millie.

She was down at the end of the bar, just walking into the place. And she looked amazing. More than amazing — great.

She noticed me and headed my way.

Her white hair dropped down out of a small blue hat that fell soft around her face like a frame. Her dress was loose and flowing but casual, made out of what looked like silk. It came up to just above her knee and flowed around her like a wave. The top of it was tied off with a long blue silk sailor knot.

She looked like no sailor this ex-Marine had ever seen.

As she walked down the length of the bar, she got more than her share of looks. Ada saw me looking at something, then swiveled her head only slightly to see what was coming. She looked back at me. "Have fun, sailor."

I looked at her. "Marine."

"I know." She took the last sip of her beer. "I like to piss you off."

With that, Ada picked her cane up off the bar and shuffled out herself, taking a long look at the coming storm as she left.

Millie walked up as Toots cleared Ada's glass and wiped down the bar fast as a man clearing the way for a queen.

"Hi, stranger." She looked at me, not Toots, but it didn't faze him a bit.

"What can I get for you, darlin'?"

She smiled at him and sat, then looked at my glass full of amber. "I'll have what he's having."

Toots' smile cracked just a bit, only enough that I could tell, but it did crack a bit. Before he had to decide to tell her no, I jumped in. "I'll cover it, Toots. No problem."

Toots looked at me and smiled. "A true gentleman."

And it was going to cost me. You didn't just get bottles of Jameson during Prohibition, there were costs involved. And even if that bottle would flow free for me for as long as time, if anyone else wanted a bit of it, he'd charge.

But I didn't worry about it because in the end, Jim was going to pay for it. Expenses, all right. Millie was smart.

She raised her glass and offered a toast. "To things." She had a look in her eye like she knew exactly what "things" meant.

I didn't. "To things." Or maybe I did.

We both drank and her eyes went wide. "Oh… this is good."

In Prohibition, everybody got used to drinking anything from rotgut to bathtub gin. The hazards of the time. So anytime anyone ran into the real stuff — and Jameson was beyond the real stuff — people stood up and took note.

And drank it.

"I know." Even the split in my lip didn't bother me as it went down. I started to get warm. Maybe a little more warm than five drinks of Jameson would account for.

"So…" she started.

"So…" I finished.

"So," she took a big breath, "I guess it's time for business. What do you want to know?"

# Chapter 28

I LIKED HER GETTING to the point.

Liked it a lot. Liked a lot about her as she sat there in her blue sailor outfit, still with the hat, and with the brown eyes that shifted between hard, and then soft at the blink of an eye.

I motioned for Toots to top off her drink, and mine while he was at it. Then like she said, we got down to business. "What do you know about Carlo?"

"Besides that he looks like a monkey?"

I snorted. I wanted to laugh but choked it off.

"What?"

"Nothing. I had the same thought myself." Then I smiled. I actually smiled. "Okay, so he's a monkey."

"He's also not a good person to be around. I've talked with some of the girls from the Santorini. He's a dictator."

"Does he hit them?"

She looked down at her drink like she didn't want to answer. But she did. Resigned. "Yeah." She looked back up at me, her eyes still going between hard and soft, trying to figure out where they wanted to land. They landed soft. "Holly, actually."

Okay.

"They dated when Holly was at the Viceroy."

"Wait, Holly was at the Viceroy? When?"

Millie thought for a second. "It was a year and a half ago. Right before Mother left to open her diner."

"Wait, I thought Mother's worked there for sixteen years?"

Holly shrugged her shoulders. "Mostly. She left to open the diner, a small place. But she came back to the Viceroy within a month."

"A month?" Then I could feel it all slipping away, the conversation about Holly. I Shouldn't have asked about Mother. Too much Jameson. I was getting downright chatty.

Millie shrugged her shoulders. "She said it didn't work out. It got busted up real bad the night before it was supposed to open. We were all gonna go down there to, you know, congratulate her, but… she never opened. She and her son had all their money in that place. Everything she'd saved working for the System."

I felt sorry for Mother but I needed to get this back to Holly. "What about—"

"And of course the cops, they didn't do a thing." Millie was getting mad, and I'm not sure if it was over Mother, or the cops themselves. "She had no more money so she couldn't pay them anything to actually *do* something. So we all offered to chip in so she could pay them off — so they actually *would* do something. But she said she didn't want it. Said it was the diner around the corner did it. That's what she said. And if she raised a stink, they'd probably come in and kill *her* the next time." Millie looked right at me. "You believe that? Over a diner?"

I'd heard worse.

She was all worked up and I had to get her back on track. "You were saying about Holly, though."

Then Millie looked like she was hit by a board. "Holly…" She'd forgotten. She froze in time there, at the bar, until in a shimmering second, a tear formed in her eye, and fell. Then another. Then a lot.

I wasn't sure where it was all coming from. I guess she knew Holly, but… "Millie…"

She tried to hold it in, but couldn't. Her face twisted in pain, then the tears came even harder and she dropped her head into her hands.

"It's okay…"

An older guy in a gray suit on the other side of Millie looked at me, wondering what I'd said, wondering what kind of a heel I was. He wasn't a regular so the hell with him.

"I know she's dead, but…." It came out almost as a whisper through the quiet sobs. "We heard about it this morning. I don't know what I'm going to do."

"You're going to be fine."

"I don't mean about me, I mean about—" Her voice stopped in her hands like she'd choked it off.

"About what?" It wasn't making much sense.

The sobs stopped and everything else seemed to, too. Then there was nothing from her.

"What?"

She pulled out a small handbag I didn't even know she had, and pulled out a small lace handkerchief. It had small embroidered yellow daisies on it, which I never would have expected.

"I'm sorry…" her voice was slightly choked but she struggled against it, pulling her face from her hands and wiping at her eyes. "I knew her, that's all. Sorry." Then she grabbed her glass and drained the rest of it in one go.

I nodded to Toots, who had been watching the waterworks out of the corner of his eye. He filled her glass, and mine, and left quick to let me clean up the mess.

"What do you have to do about Holly?" She had me curious. I wondered if she knew about the boxes. Or if there was something else. Maybe she was in on the pics, knew about them. "She ever tell you about any black-and-blue parties?"

Millie quick-dabbed at her eyes with her handkerchief and by the time the handkerchief was gone from them, her eyes were back to that subtle hardness she had had before. Like she was dealing with a John. "No. Nothing about that. Well…" She was back to hesitating. Again looking at me, trying to decide exactly what to tell me. Then she spilled it. "She said she had to be away for a couple days. For Carlo."

"When?"

"Three days ago."

"Did she say where it was? Where she was going?"

"No." Her eyes cleared back to soft again. "She didn't tell me a thing. She said it was better if I didn't know."

"Was she afraid of Carlo?"

Millie looked at her drink and her upper lip twitched. There were fine hairs on it that glowed golden. Soft. Finer than silk. "Yeah."

"Did she tell you about any pictures?"

Millie looked up at me, a question in her eyes. "No."

I believed her.

"What pictures?"

"I found some pictures in her place."

"You were there?"

"It's what I do. And when someone like Jim asks you to do something, it's a good idea to be thorough. So I found some pictures. It was of girls getting hit. Slugged." I didn't tell her that one of the guys doing the hitting was her man from the yacht.

Millie looked at me but there was no surprise in her eyes.

I looked right back at her. "You knew."

Millie got angry. "I told her not to do it." But the anger wasn't at me. It was at Holly. "She had done it a few times, over the last eight months. She only did it for the money. It was to stake her and—" Millie stopped abrupt. Then started back up like nothing had happened, "…and let her get the hell out of this place. Out of LA. She was going to maybe head back to her home, she wasn't sure. And now she's dead."

The hardness was back in Millie's eyes and it was sheened over with anger. She held the handkerchief like she was going to strangle it.

"She had to have told you where it was. The place."

"She never said a thing. She'd just come back after a few days and I could tell it had been rough. But she also had a lot of extra money." Millie looked off at the bottles behind the bar, like she was looking into a dream. "She was the one told me to do the same. Save up and get the hell out of here." She reached to her glass and knocked back the rest of it like a pro.

Toots looked at me, a question in his eye. I shook my head. She didn't need any more.

Millie looked around. "Nice place, huh? I never saw you here before." Nice change of subject.

Funny thing was, I was wondering the same thing. This place was practically home to me and I'd never seen her before. Not that I doubted her, but, "I'm here pretty regular. How often are you in?"

She swiveled her head from the bottles to look at me with her light brown eyes and didn't talk. It's like she was looking at me for the first time, again, her brown eyes searching into me for something. Then her face softened, slowly, like she just wanted to be there. Talking with somebody. A friend, maybe.

Somebody. Somebody that didn't want something from her.

"Actually, not a lot." She looked around the saloon again but this time slowly, like she was actually looking. At the people at the bar, then behind her in the booths against the wall. Everyone looked like they were having a good time. Then she looked back at me. "Coming to a place like this costs money. And like Holly told me, I'm saving mine."

I nodded.

"Does that surprise you, Mr. Detective?"

"I like to save a bit now and then myself. But it's a little harder nowadays."

She sat there silent in her blue hat, and I wasn't sure what else to say.

"I'm going to get the hell out of… all of it." She tapped the side of her empty glass and it made a tinging sound. Light, low, and almost lost in the great sounds of the place.

Maybe there were a lot of empty things in her life. I figured one more question wouldn't hurt. "You getting close to going?"

She hesitated for a moment. "Almost enough." Then she looked at me. Now there was a strong hardness in her eyes, like she was going to get what she wanted. "So — your place or mine."

# Chapter 29

VINCE SAT IN THE back of his car, looking out the back window as a very rare, hard Los Angeles rain fell. There were occasional flashes of lightning but no thunder.

Then what he was waiting for eventually happened — Devin came out of O'Hanlon's Deli. But he wasn't alone, he had a girl with him. Devin and the girl made a dash across the street, through the rain, and to his car.

Vince had been following Devin all day, and when he got to the warehouse, Vince almost went in himself to take care of Devin. But then the big guy went in ahead of him.

Unfortunately Devin walked out of it, and Vince tailed him right to here. He had to think of something to take care of Devin, but that was the funny thing. With all this time out in the car waiting, Vince's imagination had a chance to air out and a plan had started to form.

Vince looked at the girl he was with but couldn't make out who she was. But she looked familiar. The bright white hair caught him.

Vince tucked himself in the corner of his car so he wouldn't be seen.

As Devin's car passed, Vince eased himself to the side window just in time to see a breeze push back the blue hat of the woman in the passenger seat.

It was Millie.

And that wasn't good all.

She knew Baldy.

And definitely not good that she was with Devin. He'd put two and two together and talk to Baldy. Not good at all. Especially when Carlo was just about to put the bite on Baldy — using all the photos they had of him.

Devin was a problem.

Vince had another thing he had to take care of tonight, but as he got to thinking of Devin, an idea came to him. A good idea.

But that left Millie. After talking with Devin, she was a loose end. A loose end that Carlo — and he — couldn't afford.

And then a smile came to Vince. Like Carlo always told him — if life gave you lemons, make money off of them.

Vince crawled into the front and followed Devin.

And Millie.

Millie was going to meet an old friend.

A very rich old friend, who was definitely going to like seeing her again.

A lot.

# Chapter 30

I DROVE AWAY FROM Toots' confused.

Women were in the saloons, they were smoking, and now apparently — they were asking men if they wanted to take them home.

Well, the hell with that.

Maybe it was male pride, or maybe it was wanting to get on some kind of solid ground, but either way, I was going to take control.

So I took her to my place.

And as soon as she walked in, Millie opened her mouth. "This is cute."

Cute. She said it was cute.

As we walked into my apartment, I saw nothing cute. It was a single room with a kitchen table pushed against the far window, two chairs on either side of it. The living area consisted of nothing more than a soft chair in the corner to the right, a bureau just behind the door, and a Murphy bed tucked up into a two-doored cabinet set into the wall to the left.

In other words — nothing cute.

The kitchen was thankfully through a small doorway to the

left of the table, otherwise she probably would have labeled that "cute," too.

She must have seen the look in my eye. That, and the twin .45s in shoulder holsters after I took off my coat. "I mean," she took another look around, "manly. It definitely looks manly."

This was off to a great start. "I'll get a us a drink."

Millie took off her blue hat, and her bottle-white hair looked out of place in my place. It was — womanly. Definitely womanly. In a soft... very nice way. It had been a long time.

She stared at me. "What are you looking at?"

Silent lightning flashed from the window.

I ripped my eyes from her hair. "I'll get the drink."

"You do that."

I heard a smile in her voice, but I couldn't see a thing. I was already on my way to the kitchen. The window over the table showed the rain still coming down outside. A regular downpour.

In the kitchen I reached up into the upper cupboard and pulled down the bottle and two rocks glasses. It wasn't the good stuff, but it'd have to do. Luckily, I had gotten a new block of ice so I opened the icebox and chipped off a few pieces and loaded them in the glasses.

I walked out into the room and, unfortunately, she was in the chair nearest the kitchen door.

That was my seat.

I held in what I wanted to say, because I was a gentleman, and sat down in the other chair. I could see into my kitchen. I didn't like that. But I could see her, in my chair, in her smooth silk sailor dress. That, I had to admit, was not so bad.

The rain continued to pour outside.

I poured us each a drink and offered her a glass. "It's not the good stuff."

She looked past the glass at me. "Oh, I think it will be."

Then she winked at me.

She was doing it again. Trying to take the lead. This was not going how it was supposed to go, so I grabbed my glass and drank it.

Then she drank hers.

We both looked hungry for more, squared off across my small kitchen table, the rain still falling outside the window next to us. She pushed her glass toward me. "I don't know about you, but I'll certainly have another."

I looked at her, ready to throttle her. "Certainly."

I filled the glasses and we both drank again, our eyes not leaving each other. It wasn't attraction or anything else other than a sheer battle for control.

I poured two more and drank mine, a half second before she got hers down. We both slammed our glasses down on the table at the same time, Millie smiling at me like a kid who'd just hit a home run.

The hell with this. I got up and walked to her, picked her up by her blue silk shoulders, and kissed her.

It wasn't soft and it wasn't nice but it damn sure felt good. She must have liked it, too, because she took it.

"Oh… that was nice."

"Yeah?" I was still angry over everything, but I was definitely thawing.

"Yeah." Then she pulled my face down to her hard and kissed me right back, then finished it off with a small bite to my lower lip.

The hell with that.

I let go of her and walked to the wall, then yanked the Murphy bed down with a thud I knew was going to piss off the old man below me. Screw him.

Millie walked straight up to me, pulled my face down again and planted a kiss on me that lasted for a full five minutes. It was hot, and wet, and made me forget if anyone was in control.

Neither of us came up for air until I finally broke, took a breath, then remembered a few things about how this was supposed to go, and started kissing her on the neck.

That seemed to do something, because she let out a moan that half-sounded like a cry.

Then she pushed me down onto the bed.

I bounced hard and she fell on top of me.
Then the night got interesting.
One hell of a lot more interesting.

# Chapter 31

MILLIE HAD TO GET to work in the morning and so did I. So I took her home. Neither one of us were the share-a-morning-cup-of-joe type.

It was three o'clock, the dead of the night when I pulled up in front of Millie's apartment building. It was one of those large ones on Wilshire, in a neighborhood that was something at one time but was a little less of it now. It wasn't a bad area, but it was tired and the rent was probably cheap. Which fit in with her plan.

"Which one is yours?" I asked.

She looked up at the building and nodded toward it. "The one in the center, just over the door."

The night was still outside and it was still a little close inside the car, but the storm had blown over and all that was left was the two of us. She sat there framed by the passenger window in back of her, her hat and dress dark, but still blue in the light of the moon that had now come out between the breaking clouds. But I could see her eyes, and they looked at me.

"You know, you never really asked me about how I got into... what I do."

"I figured that was your business."

She smiled.

The air hung between us like it didn't want to move anywhere. And I guess I was content to leave it that way. She wasn't.

"I like sex."

The inside of my car felt suddenly very, very small.

And tight.

And I wanted to get out of it.

"Not in any crazy way, I just like it. Simple. So when I got to town, I found a guy who liked it, too. And we had a ball." She smiled, catching her own joke. "And I fell for him. He had a lot of money and he started to take care of things for me. Buy me nice things." She pointed up at her building. "He even got me my apartment."

They called it *treating*. I knew that much. A guy and girl get together and do what they do, and the guy gives her gifts.

"But I really did love him." The small smile she had, on thinking about it, disappeared. "I waited and waited for him, but then I finally got it that he never really loved me back. Well, he loved part of me anyways." There, she laughed. "So I found other guys. And they all liked sex, too. And like I said, so do I. And it was fun and some of them treated me nice, got me things, and it was all fun. Then one day I realized that all they wanted was not really me, but... what I could do. So..." She fanned her hands out in front of her body. "I started making real money. And that was that."

Very practical.

I shrugged my shoulders. "The only reason I'm a PI is because I knew how to use a gun. And I could hit people."

I felt something ease in the air. Inside the car.

"And do you like it?"

"If you're talking about sex, I like it just fine. If you're talking about being a PI, I like that just fine, too. Not necessarily the hitting part but... helping people. I think I'm good at it."

Millie smiled. "Then here's to doing something you're good at. And maybe even like a little." She leaned over quick, placed a light kiss on my cheek, and got out of the car.

I opened my door to walk her up, but she leaned back in on the passenger side. "It's okay, I can get myself back up. I'm a big girl." She went to leave but then leaned back in. "But I am a girl." Then she finally smiled. "And I appreciated tonight."

Then with a nod, she turned and walked up the walkway to her apartment building like she was taking the world.

I watched her until she got inside, then counted the seconds until just in time, the light came on in the center apartment over the door.

I forgot I still had my door open. I closed it, started my car, put it in gear, and drove.

I needed my bed. With nobody in it.

# Chapter 32

I WAS TIRED AS I headed back home. It had been a long day. It had been a long night.

All I was looking forward to was getting back in my bed and getting at least a little sleep before I had to get into the office.

To be honest, the night had been long, but it had been good.

I laughed. It had definitely been good.

I pulled up and found a spot right in front of my building. My luck was holding out.

The street was quiet. I looked up and my apartment faced the front of the building, like Millie's. Interesting. But I was on the corner, on the top floor. In the daylight I could see the tops of some of the king palms that lined the streets around Westlake Park a block over.

Inside, the automatic elevator was out of commission, something that happened a lot in my building, but three sets of steps isn't so much in a life that's full of them.

By the time I reached the third floor, I was reassessing my earlier view that three sets of steps wasn't much. That was hogwash. I was definitely tired.

I made my way down to the end of the hall, to the last door

on the left, my apartment. I paid a little extra for the front view, but the first apartment I had here faced out onto an alley and I figured what the heck, I was moving up in the world, why not splurge. So I took the view.

Besides, I could keep an eye on what happened out front. As much as I liked the view of the tree tops in the day, and Bartie's good old Lindberg Beacon atop City Hall, I liked keeping an eye on things even more.

I looked down, and the small brown thread I always lodged in the space between the door and jam had fallen. It lay on the red carpeted floor, right next to the jam. Somebody had been in there, or was still there waiting for me. So much for a quiet night.

I flattened my back against the wall next to the door, pulled one gun out with my right hand, then stuck the key in the lock, turned it, and pushed in on the cold black doorknob.

The door drifted open slow, until it tapped lightly into the wall on the other side of me.

Nothing came at me from inside, including gunshots, knives, or blow darts, so I figured everything was quiet. I leaned my head in to have a look.

There was nothing. Just the outline of my table and two chairs against the wall, and the silhouette of the Murphy bed still lying out from where we'd left it. Nobody sat on any of them, so I leaned in a little more and looked at the soft chair in the corner. Nothing there either.

I walked in slowly, checked the small closet, then led with my gun as I checked the kitchen. Nothing.

At least satisfied that no one else was around, unless they were hiding in the oven, I holstered my gun and locked my door.

It was stuffy inside, the closed room trapping the air and the heat from the day. And a night of fun.

I turned on the kitchen light and opened the window over the table and a small breeze brought in a little fresh air. And the far-off wail of a police siren.

Business as usual in LA.

I took off my hat and jacket and hung them on the back of my favorite chair, then went into the kitchen and got the bottle and poured myself two fingers.

I sat down as a few more sirens added to the other one, breaking the silence of the night. I thought of Millie, and it was kind of nice to have had a woman around tonight. Very nice.

I looked out at the buildings on the other side of the road as the sirens got louder and wondered just how that was going to play with all the locals sleeping — with me soon being one. It'd pass. I knocked back the two fingers as the Lindberg Beacon did its turn around the LA sky out front of me and I thought of Bartie and wondered how many airplanes were right now heading toward that light, and their own deaths.

I laughed.

Even more sirens wove in with the sounds of the other ones and they were getting close. It was a little odd.

I turned to my bed. The sheets were still rumpled, the pillows piled at the head of the bed. I pulled the pile of pillows apart — and a bloody head stared back at me.

A woman, eyes closed and covered in blood, and my drink nearly came back up to see the light of day.

Or the black of night, as it was now.

The sirens got near and I had a very bad feeling about all of this.

The head was bloody but I recognized the dark curls that held tight to it. Like the fashion five years ago.

It was the third girl in the pictures.

Carlo had gotten to her.

Her full face sat there in my bed, looking at me as if I was the one to blame.

Then all those cop cars I heard pulled to a halt outside my building, the sirens still screaming. A bunch of car doors slammed shut.

A lot of doors.

And a lot of cops came out of them.

They'd be up the steps and in my door in probably about

fifteen seconds.

I cut the light, grabbed my hat and jacket, and got myself out of there as quick as I could.

There were enough cops outside I was sure they'd have every exit covered. Front, back, and sideways — everything.

Now a lot of people don't like planning. Me, I love it. It's what's kept me alive all these years.

In the Marines you always knew two things — what you were setting out to do, and how you'd handle things if it all went south. And in the Marines, in war, everything went south. A lot. So you plan.

You get ideas.

So when I first looked at apartments in LA I paid attention to the view, but I also paid attention to other things.

It just so happened that there were three sets of stairs in this building, one up the middle and one at each end. And as it happened, the middle one led to the roof. The only problem was that it was the same set of stairs the cops would be coming up to theoretically come to my apartment. Because if you leave a head in somebody's bed, of course you're going to call the cops.

A nice joke by Carlo and Vince, no doubt.

I'd have to repay them.

I closed my apartment door behind me, then ran for my life down the red carpeted hallway.

It was like I was a kid again, the wind thundering across my ears as I ran light as air, my feet barely hitting the carpet.

Already there were voices coming from below, and heavy feet attacking the wood stairs along with them.

I made it to the stairs just as the first of the thundering hooves hit the second floor, and I ran up the next two sets of stairs, carefully avoiding each place I knew there was a creak. Because I had planned.

I got to the darkened top of the stairs, then quietly pushed through the gray metal door to the roof.

Up top, a breeze drifted across the tar-papered roof as if

nothing was going on in the world.

I wouldn't have long.

The two fire escapes from the place would be covered, that was for sure, as well as the back. Nothing could get in or out of the building. Which is why I planned on actually getting out of the building — five buildings down.

Another reason I chose my place was because all the buildings near it were the same three stories tall, and all of their roofs stretched out in front of me to the west. Some walls around their tops were taller than others, but I could make them. I had to.

I ran to the edge of my building and the small, two-foot wall around it. I timed it perfectly and hit the top of the wall with my right foot, and launched myself to the next roof.

The next building was only four feet away and I made it clean. By the time I reached the fifth building, my legs were jelly but they held up. Barely. I had made it.

I found the roof door leading down into the building, had to pick it to get through, but got out of there before anyone thought to get to the roof of my building.

I was down the stairs and out onto the next street in another ten seconds, and safely away from any cops.

I continued up the street only long enough to get to an alley, then made my way through a few more dirty and dusty ones for a couple more blocks until I was well away from my apartment.

And I had a chance to think.

The head was a message from Carlo. I figured I'd need to give him a message of my own.

Soon.

# Chapter 33

I KNOCKED ON THE smooth white door of number five and it was four o'clock.

The Trudy Motel was not much to look at. A courtyard place on 7th about three blocks from my office. It had a decidedly Old English feel, with white stucco walls, dark wood beams crossing everywhere on its side, and a wall above the entry drive designed to look like the entry to a castle.

It probably played well to the tourists that came to LA, looking for their piece of Hollywood, but the place was built maybe ten years ago and it had started to show its age.

All the dark beams on the walls had a layer of dirt and dust on the tops of them. The white walls were chipped in places and weren't so white anymore. And the walkway around the second level of rooms that all faced into the small paved courtyard wobbled and warped like something that was built in Shakespeare's time. In other words, it was the perfect place to hide.

Which is why Charlie was there.

When he started to work for me, I set Charlie up here so he'd have a place to stay, seeing as how his old man had thrown him out of their own home. The Trudy wasn't much, but it was a place for a kid who had nowhere else to go.

The door to number five, second floor, swung open and the head of a confused and clearly still half-asleep Charlie poked out. "Mr. Devin?" From what I could see, inside the dark room behind him looked like a fifteen year old lived there. Which he was. And it did.

"Sorry to bother you, Charlie. Can I come in?"

He looked at me with his blue eyes trying to wake up. "Uh, sure." He still stood there looking at me, right in my way.

"It's customary to open the door first."

"Right." And he did.

Charlie ran to a pair of dungarees sitting in the far corner of the room – a corner that was only ten feet away. He pulled the dungarees on in a hurry, his eyes not meeting mine until they covered his plain white drawers. More or less properly attired, he looked at me. "Sorry about the mess."

The mess. It looked like any other room of a fifteen year old, including mine when I was living back on the farm in Michigan. But at least Charlie didn't own too much, so the mess was kept to a minimum by default.

"Don't worry about it. I've seen worse, including my own."

Charlie gave a half smile, but then walked around the tiny room, picking up the few pieces of clothes left on the floor and bed, tossing them into one of the three drawers of the beat-up black wood bureau in the other far corner of the place. Beyond the small room was a small area in back with the bathroom to the left, and a counter and sink to the right. Next to the sink sat a hot plate with a single, dented silver pan on top.

From the look of it, the pan had been used for a week, and not cleaned too strenuously for most of it.

The smell was a little ripe in the place for my liking, but keeping the door open was not an option.

I walked over to the left to the lone window into the place, reached to the bottom of the yellowed roller shade, and cracked the window a bit. I'd risk anyone hearing what we were saying, to let in at least a little fresh air to the place. Not that there was much of a breeze blowing outside, but when imminent death is close, you try drastic measures.

Charlie stood on the other side of the bed. It was a little awkward, the two of us standing, so I invited Charlie to take a load off and motioned to the bed. "Go on, have a seat."

He did, as he pulled on a wrinkled white dress shirt to completely cover himself.

"I'm in a bit of jam, Charlie."

Charlie looked at me, young concern in his eyes. "What happened?"

I almost laughed. The kid actually cared. A thing a little different in my neck of the woods. "Well…" I wondered how to start it exactly; the kid was still only fifteen. But throwing caution to the wind, I figured I'd hit him with it straight. That always seemed to serve me well. "The cops think I killed someone."

Charlie looked at me, standing in his room at four in the morning. I think maybe his caring had met its limit.

"Don't worry," I began, "I didn't do it."

The tension in Charlie's eyes fell. He wore his feelings on his face. I hoped he never took up poker.

"The full story is, I got back to my apartment a little bit ago, and there was…" I paused, not sure if I should tell him, but in for a penny, in for a pound. And if he was going to continue to work for me, he'd better toughen up a little to what life in LA could throw at you. "There was a head in my bed."

Charlie didn't move, frozen there. Then his mouth opened just a bit like he was going to say something, then it shut again. Then it opened. "It's the case that you're working on. The one with the prostitutes getting chopped up, right?"

Okay, I'll add keeping informed to his list of skills. "Yeah."

"Do you know who did it?"

"Yeah."

"Do you want me to help you get him?" Charlie was up and pulling at the dresser drawer again. He pulled out a pair of black socks, at the same time looking around for his shoes.

"No, I don't want you in the middle of any of this. Bella would have my hide."

Charlie stood up after getting his socks on. He looked at me like a kid who'd just had a Tommy gun pulled from his hands. "But I want to help."

"And you will." I walked around the end of the bed to face him. "I'm going to get a room right here at the Trudy, but away from you. I want to keep you as much away from this as possible."

Charlie nodded.

"I'll need you to get a few things from the office, but they'll probably be keeping an eye on the place. So I have an idea."

I told Charlie the idea.

He seemed to like it.

# Chapter 34

CHARLIE RODE ON A bike, straight up 7th.

Well, not straight up, but more on the edge between the cars running to his left, and the ones parked to his right. Beyond the parked cars was Westlake Park. He was near the office.

The tight white pants he wore rode up on his butt as he pushed on the pedals, while the too-small, white delivery jacket felt like a straitjacket. But Charlie played his part well as he rode — Mr. Devin's life depended on it. Although Charlie was wondering about his own life at the moment. It had been six years since he'd even been on a bike.

That was when his old man had run over his first and only bike. The old man came home from work — drunk, as usual — ran over the bike, crushing it, then ran upstairs to smack Charlie around because he'd left it out. That was the first time Charlie had run into the woods to stay. It was just a couple of nights, but he found from there on out, his ability to run on his own two feet was a lot better than relying on any bike. Or anyone else to save him.

Until Mr. Devin.

The plan was simple — get to the office, get two boxes out of one of Mr. Devin's safes, and take them back to him at the hotel. And stay away from the office after that.

It was almost noon, which was part of the plan. The bike was a delivery bike, with a huge white box sitting on the front of it. Two feet tall, two feet deep, and three feet wide, it was tied to the front fender and had a large red wall painted on the front, with letters spelling out *Chinese Wall Restaurant* above it. *Best food in town* was painted below, and judging by the smell of what was inside — chop suey and egg rolls — Charlie figured it was pretty right. Although he'd never had Chinese food in his life.

Charlie got the bike, and the white delivery boy's outfit, from Mr. Park at the Chinese Wall. Mr. Park owed Mr. Devin a favor, at least that's what Mr. Devin had told Charlie. But from the way Charlie saw it, the ten dollars he gave Mr. Park seemed to do more than the favor.

Charlie had it down pretty good, balancing the box on the front of the bike and keeping himself from dying. Until a car door shot out in front of him.

A guy in a tan straw hat got out from his car, and his eyes went wide as Charlie bore down on him.

Charlie jerked the handlebars, still holding onto the box, and shot directly into traffic.

"Hey!"

The guy in front of him didn't matter anymore because he wasn't there anymore — a black delivery truck was. Heading straight for him in the middle of 7th.

Brakes screeched and a car horn blasted from in back of him. Charlie guessed it was the tan Packard he had just passed. Nice car, but big enough to kill him. And the truck was even bigger.

The delivery truck hit his brakes and swerved, two tires exploding out.

This wasn't good at all. The only thing Mr. Devin had said was don't stick out. That's why the delivery outfit.

Of course, Charlie wondered how a big kid like him, dressed all in white on a Chinese delivery bike, didn't stick out. But he left that to Mr. Devin. He was the smart one.

And Charlie was about to be dead.

Then, as if nothing had happened, he cleared the intersection at 7th and Carol — and shot down Carol as he left probably fifty car and truck horns blaring behind him.

"Whoo!!" He felt like a million bucks.

Then he cut into the first alley to the right, right in back of the office building that held John Devin Investigations. Their home.

Bella sat at her desk in what Charlie knew was her favorite white blouse. It had little stitching at the end of the collars like doilies. But she was no doily. "You're late."

She looked at Charlie like he'd committed a mortal sin, and in her book, lateness was. Especially for a kid who had gotten the job by the skin of his teeth. This job was the only thing he had, and Bella's look hurt him. "It's okay." Charlie, awkward and now nervous, tried to put the big white box down on Bella's desk and her face went even colder. He immediately set it down on the floor in front of him. "I'm undercover for Mr. Devin."

"What?" Bella smiled at him like she was about to cut him to pieces. "Like a G-man?"

"Yeah." Charlie looked into Mr. Devin's private office to make sure the coast was clear. It was empty. Charlie went back to the reception area and Bella looked like she was about to hit him.

She always intimidated Charlie. Mostly because she... knew what she was doing. "Mr. Devin's in it bad."

Bella listened to everything Charlie told her, but her expression didn't change too much along the way. Charlie wasn't sure if she believed him or thought he was lying.

Then her brown eyes softened, just a bit. "You need the combination to the safe?"

Good. Charlie smiled. "Mr. Devin changed it."

"He did, huh?"

"Yeah, and he gave me the right one."

Bella didn't look too pleased. As in very not pleased. And Charlie wondered if it was because he had the combination and she didn't?

To make her happy, Charlie opened the white box on the floor and the thick smell of chop suey and egg rolls came drifting out. It was amazing. He set the two white cartons of food on Bella's desk. And he smiled.

She didn't. "What am I supposed to do with those?" She looked at them, sitting on her desk, like they were a couple of dead animals.

"Eat them. It's lunch, for you. From Mr. Devin."

Bella's look got even worse. "That ain't American food."

Charlie was confused. "He said you loved it."

"He lied. Playing a practical joke on me." Bella pushed the white cartons as far to the edge of her desk as she could without actually pushing them off. "You can get these away from me."

Inside Mr. Devin's office, Charlie walked up to the big black safe against the wall with "Washington" written across the bottom of its door in gold script. It looked like it was made for a president.

There was a brass handle on the side and a brass dial just next to it. Charlie pulled out a small scrap of paper that Mr. Devin had written the combination on — a five-number combination — and it took him three tries before he tried the handle and the safe opened.

Charlie had never seen the inside of a safe before. This one had rows of large cubbyholes all along the left side of it, and a large open area to the right that looked like you could hang a jacket in.

The safe was completely empty except for two shoe boxes, one yellow and one black, and a white envelope, all in the cubbies to the left. Charlie took all three, then brought them out into the reception area and put them into the big white box.

Bella wouldn't look at him.

"Mr. Devin said not to come back today, and maybe tomorrow. He said there were probably cops watching the place."

Bella still didn't look up at him. "There is. He's out on Seventh, and was there when I got in this morning."

Charlie felt bad. He wanted to say something to her, to get her to at least look at him. But he knew it wouldn't do any good.

When Bella got mad, she kind of didn't talk anymore. So Charlie headed for the door.

"Go out the side."

Charlie looked up at her and she was looking at him. Her eyes were still a little hard but there was some softness in them now. "You take care."

Charlie nodded. And left.

He opened the side door onto Carol and just as he hit the heat of the sun, a hand grabbed his arm. Hard.

"Hey kid, I told you to stop."

Charlie looked around and the guy in the tan straw hat stood here, his hand an iron grip on Charlie's arm. He was the same height as Charlie, and his green eyes tore into him like broken glass.

"Do you know what you just did back there?"

Charlie held the white box in his other arm, and hoped the guy didn't hear the sound of the boxes moving around inside.

But it wasn't exactly a guy that held him, it was a cop. A detective.

He wore a wrinkled suit the color of desert dirt and Charlie could see his gun tucked into his waistband. It had a black handle on it, that's all he saw as the cop jerked at him again to get Charlie to look him in the eye.

Charlie did. "I'm sorry, sir." Charlie really wanted to say something else — he had had enough of his old man grabbing him just like this, but he kept calm. Didn't want to call any attention to himself, at least not any more than he already had. "I was just going along and you opened up your door."

"You weren't lookin', kid!"

"You're right, I wasn't." It was the stance Charlie always took with his old man.

"You could have killed me. And a lot of other people."

The cop's fingers dug into Charlie's arm. It hurt a lot.

"What were you doing, anyway?"

"Delivering lunch, sir. To the dressmaker downstairs." It's the only thing Charlie could think of. And he hoped the cop didn't decide to check.

Then the cop seemed to notice the white box Charlie carried in his other arm. The cop nodded to it. "What kind of food is it?" He looked hungry.

"Chinese, sir." Charlie couldn't breathe.

"Any good?"

"No, sir." Charlie finally took a breath, and forced himself not to look away from the cop's eyes. "Can't eat it myself. It ain't American."

The cop looked at the box, then back at Charlie.

"You better watch yourself. I see you again riding like that, I'll personally take that bike and smash it."

"Yes, sir."

The cop let go of Charlie's arm, and the pain still spiked through it. He knew he'd have bruises. He always did. Why would this time be any different?

The cop walked back up the sidewalk and Charlie got to the alley, got on the bike with the box, and rode for thirty minutes straight until he knew the cop was nowhere around.

Then he headed back to the Trudy, and Mr. Devin.

He wouldn't mention anything about the cop.

It didn't mean anything.

Getting bruised never did.

# Chapter 35

I WASN'T AN IDIOT.

After Charlie brought me the two boxes, I took a taxi down to Central Station, made a quick visit to Billie, and dropped off the two boxes in a new storage locker.

Number eight. I liked the luck of it.

I held the white envelope out because I needed to do something with it. But as I was closing up the locker, that little voice in the back of my head thought maybe it was a good idea to pull out all five pics of the tall bald guy and leave them in there. I guess I agreed because I pulled all of them out of the white envelope, put them on top of the two shoe boxes, and closed the locker tight.

The rest of the pics I took to a photographer friend who could keep his mouth shut, and had him shoot dupes of all of them. That would take a bit, so during that time I made a couple calls. The photographer charged me extra for the calls.

The first call was to Jim, to bring him up to date. At least as far up to date as I wanted to get him. I didn't want to let him know Carlo was involved, not yet anyway. I was sure he was the one, along with Vince, but I wanted to make sure I had everything tight before I approached Jim. But it's also not a bad idea to drop a few hints along the way, so I let slip that someone in his organization might be doing a few things they shouldn't. Just in case Carlo started trying to make the same accusations — of me. What with a dead head in my bed and all.

So I dropped my hints, told Jim things were progressing, and that I should have something for him soon.

I hoped.

The other call I made was to Bella. We had a code, if ever I was worried that the phone lines were tapped I'd call and ask for a Mr. Bennett. Bella would take down the return number I gave her, then hike over to the accountant across the hall to call me back. It wasn't exactly sophisticated, but it got the job done.

It took her two minutes to call. I picked it up on the first ring. "What kept you?"

"I had to go to the little girl's room."

Bella called it that. She was anything but. "I need you to run an errand for me."

I heard a snort at the other end of the line. "Why don't you get your new best friend to do it. He did so well delivering lunch."

I almost laughed. She was jealous. Unbelievable. And he was the one supposed to be a kid. "Do *you* want to be out riding a bicycle?"

"I was a girl once."

"I find that hard to believe."

There was silence on the other end of the line.

"Bella?"

"I'm just waiting here until you're done with the wisecracks. Are you done yet?"

"I'm done."

"All right, what do you want me to do?"

I told her.

After I finished with Bella, I picked up the two sets of snaps the photographer pushed across the desk to me — the originals and the dupes. I nodded to him and put the originals back into the white envelope and pocketed the dupes. Then I paid him.

Then I dropped off the originals, along with the white envelope, back with Billie at the storage lockers. By that time, it was past six and I had a few hours to kill.

Unfortunately I killed some of it thinking. About Carlo. I wanted to kill him.

Thinking of that girl's head in my place, lying there on the bed, made my stomach turn. What he did to her.

There are guys like that. I'd seen one in the war.

He had been in our company, and we'd all kept clear of him. He had a look in his eyes. One night after a raid, nobody realized it but he dragged a body back to the trenches and set up shop in a little cul-de-sac. There were plenty of those cul-de-sacs in the trenches, usually where you stored supplies and things. But the one he picked was way off away from everybody. So he could do what he wanted.

The corporal did a head count after we got back and nobody had seen the guy go down, so the corporal went off to find him. No man of his was going to go AWOL.

The corporal found him, butchering the fresh dead body. The guy had taken it apart simple, clean, and careful. Wore its entrails wrapped around his neck like a mink stole.

The corporal surprised the guy, and got a knife in the gut for his troubles.

We heard the scream across the trenches.

It took the rest of us to bring the guy down. His name was Harry. From Chicago. Maybe he was a butcher back there.

He didn't make it out of that trench. We took care of him. The way I look at it, we probably saved a few people back in Chicago with that one.

If he'd ever have gone back home.

So the way I was thinking of it, Carlo wasn't making it out of this.

At all.

# Chapter 36

I WALKED INTO THE notions store on the corner of Broadway and 5th. What better place to call the police.

I got in the phone booth they had in the corner, then called LAPD headquarters and asked for Cardon. I was lucky. He was in.

"This is Cardon."

"So did you get my little gift?"

"Devin?"

"Yeah. Did you look at it?" I heard some rustling, probably reaching for the photos. There were also mixed, muffled voices in the background, other detectives. Cardon lowered his voice. "Yeah, I got them."

"Do you recognize any of the girls? As in three of them? Holly, Helen Humphries, and whoever belonged to that head in my bed?"

"And to the rest of her beneath it."

"They left the rest of her, too?"

"And the saw."

Well. "I guess that'll teach me to check under my bed when I get home."

"And there was another, this morning."

"You mean not the one in my bed?"

"Yeah, another. Back out by the warehouses. That's seven now. You gotta come in, Devin. They're all out for you. Or if you want me to come get you, I will."

"Not going to happen, Cardon. I'm getting close to getting to whoever did it. And in case you were wondering, it wasn't me."

"Of course it wasn't you."

"Really? You believe me? That was easy."

"I know a frame when I see it."

"Good for you. And in case your gut isn't enough, that's what the pics are for. The girls were involved in a little extra-curricular activity — not involving me. I think something happened."

"Of course something happened; they're dead."

"I'm finding exactly what."

"Mind letting me in on anything?"

"I don't think my employer would like it."

"Who is it — Carlo or Jim?"

"Who said it was either?"

Cardon sighed on the other end of the phone. "The girls had arrests, all of them bailed out by the same lawyer. The System's lawyer."

"Hmm…"

"My guess is Jim. He's your friend, right?"

I didn't answer. It was complicated.

"Devin—""

"Look, Cardon, I just wanted you to know I didn't do it. It's not good proof, what you have there, but it's something."

"Who set it up?"

I looked out the small glass pane in the door of the phone booth. At the counter, a small girl had a nickel's worth of candy sitting on the countertop. Her mother stood next to her holding her hand. Maybe it was the first purchase of her life. She looked happy, at least somebody was. "You know, Cardon, I have my ideas, but I'm not quite sure."

"Tell me."

I hung up the phone and didn't say goodbye. I hoped that wasn't rude.

Then I made one more call.

When I finally finished I opened the door to the phone booth. A guy stood off to the side and gave me the stink eye. Apparently he'd been waiting to get in.

Everybody was unhappy.

Except the girl at the counter. She had her candy and bounced out the front door into the sunlight beyond.

At least someone was happy in this city.

It sure as hell wasn't me.

# Chapter 37

SOMETIMES IN A CASE, you move from investigating to actually doing something about it.

That time was now.

I walked down 5th to the Cairo Hotel a few blocks away. I knew a guy.

Manny Chavez ran the boys out front who took care of people's cars. They all wore a… costume. It had a tan jacket on top, and loose, billowing tan pants below. On their feet were slippers of brown suede, with the whole package meant to look like a cross between a uniform and something out of *Arabian Nights*.

To me, the only thing it succeeded in was looking stupid. And the boys agreed.

"Manny…"

Manny stood five and a half feet to my six, had short black hair and a clean shaved face. His face held the deep tan of someone in the sun all day, was full, and had a smile on it no matter what was happening. Including wearing a ridiculous uniform. "How are you, Mr. Devin?"

"Doing great — if you have what I need?"

Three other guys, younger than Manny, milled around the

entrance to the hotel. Business it seemed, was slow.

Manny pulled up next to me, two friends sharing a secret. "I do, and I took care of it myself." He nodded to one of the boys and the kid shot off around Spring.

"How's Graciella?"

Manny brightened up. "She's singing now."

His daughter would be three. I remember when Manny had her. I was walking down Spring and he up and handed me a cigar. Didn't even know him, but his face beamed like sunshine. I thought his smile was going to split his head.

The cigar was a little iffy, but Manny? He was a good egg. "You should put her on the radio."

Manny laughed. "I think I will keep her at home."

"See Manny, between the two of us, you're the smart one."

He laughed, but I was thinking exactly that. Because I was about to do something really, really stupid.

The boy who had run off drove back in Bella's car. An old Model T that looked as new as the day it was born. Bella took care of things.

The boy got out and I tipped him a buck. Manny — I gave him five.

Manny looked down at it like it was the gold that it was. Not a lot of money flowing these days. He looked up into my eyes, his deep brown ones intent. "Thank you, Mr. Devin."

I would actually thank Jim. "Manny, you saved my life."

I got in the car and took off, thinking I was actually probably ending it.

Oh, well.

I drove up Spring, and headed straight into stupidity.

# Chapter 38

BELLA HAD DROPPED OFF the car as part of her errand.

My car was stuck at my place and if I went back to get it, the cops would get me. And there was only so much I could do taking Red Cars all day, so Bella dropped her car at the Cairo, then took the Red Car back to the office. I only hoped the cop watching the office wasn't bright enough to notice.

He probably wasn't. Nobody paid him enough.

The extra call I made at the phone booth was back to Jim. I got Carlo's address from him. His home address.

See, Carlo didn't wake up before five. And it being noon and all, there was no chance he would be anywhere but in his bed. Which was good.

The whole stupid part of this idea was in the fact that Carlo was one of the leaders of the System. I mean, I knew Jim better, and Jim had hired me to find out who was doing this to the girls, but if I was wrong, going after Carlo was not going to extend my life at all.

But honestly, it was already on the very short side.

With Carlo dropping the head off in my bed, it meant he didn't want me around. Hang all the murders on me and have me float

147

away to prison. Or if that didn't work, I was sure he would just have me killed. So either way, I was a dead man.

But I'd already been a dead man enough times in my life.

What was one more?

All the girls in the pics were accounted for. Holly, Helen, and now the plain girl were all dead. With Anna Banko the only smart one who saved herself and got away.

They were the only ones who could tell me where the room was, and tie Carlo to the murders. I suppose I could look across the country for Anna, but how long was that going to take? Long enough so that Carlo would get to be his usual impatient self and have me killed direct.

I knew what I was up against.

There was a remote possibility that the room was at his house. He was maybe stupid enough for that. But if it wasn't, I'd just convince him to tell me where it was. Telling me he did it, and writing out a confession was probably too much to ask. So I would take it in small steps. Just tell me where the room was.

Maybe I'd tie him to his own bed when I found him in it. Maybe smack him around a bit before I shoved both of my guns in his mouth and asked him where the room was.

Right; then he wouldn't be able to talk.

I'd figure it out. So many decisions.

And for the first time in this case — I was starting to feel good about them.

# Chapter 39

CARLO LIVED IN A small bungalow on the south end of Beverly Hills. Not exactly the prime area but most likely with the address, with "Beverly Hills" after it, he could still think he was with the rich people.

But as one of the lieutenants of the System, he was also not doing too bad.

The bungalow had two palm trees out front, a yard that looked like it was taken care of by other people, and a nice front of white stucco, and brown Spanish-style shutters. All in all it was not the least bit gaudy, which totally went against Carlo.

I suppose he was just trying to fit in — way above his status.

I pulled right into the drive and continued up to the side of the house. The large front window on this side of the house told me it was the living room, far away from Carlo's bedroom. Honestly, I didn't stop out on the street because I think I was looking for a confrontation with him. I think I wanted to get at it as soon as I could.

Nobody came out to greet me, so I went around to the back. If you were going to break into a house while the owner was sleeping, it was always best to do it from the back. That was house-breaking basics.

In the back there was a pool, light blue at the bottom.

A tall fence surrounded the back yard, which was thoughtful, because now I didn't have to sneak around at all. That Carlo, thinking of everything.

A small covered porch sat off the back of the house, with a solid brown wooden door leading inside.

I leaned in and checked the back window nearest me. It looked like a small living room with a blue sofa and two light orange chairs — and nobody in them.

I pulled out my picks and was in the house in a flash.

Into the kitchen, specifically.

It was done in green walls and a lighter green countertop, with a white tile floor to I guess, add some light to the place.

I did a quick check and the only door in the kitchen led into a pantry. I guess I was hoping for a set of stairs down into a basement where the secret room was, but no such luck. The place wasn't that big, and if the living room was to the left, the bedrooms had to be to the right.

Curtains were drawn everywhere, the sign of a night owl.

I quietly, and quickly, peeked into the living room that wrapped around the front of the house and into the side room that I had looked in from the back. Still nobody anywhere. At least I was alone so far.

On the way to the living room I passed a hall that headed to the other side of the house, so I went back to it. There I'd find Carlo.

The weight of my guns felt good in my hands, both from the loaded magazines they carried, and because they would hit harder when I smashed them into Carlo's head.

There was always the idea that this may not work out the way I wanted, but as the Marines taught me, it's better to at least do something. Otherwise you just remain a target.

The small hallway was dim, with no windows itself, but there was a small bit of light coming into it from three open doors along it. The bathroom first, I would guess, on my left, then two doors at the end of the hall that would most likely, lead into two bedrooms. With the bathroom on the left, my guess was the larger bedroom was on the right.

I walked slow and careful up the hallway.

I fully expected to hear Carlo snoring, I don't know why. Maybe because he looked like a goon. But everything was quiet, and something in me started thinking it was too quiet.

I looked into the green and white bathroom and it was clear, then kept walking up the hall.

A little ways from the two doors, I held to the right side of the hall so I could get at least a little angle into the bedroom on the left. In the dimness there looked to be a desk and that made me feel a little better. Nobody else in the house except Carlo. Unless he had a guest in there.

I got to the bedroom doorway on the right and listened from outside. There was no sound of sleeping, no breathing, not even a small stir. Way too quiet.

I walked in — to an empty bed.

Carlo wasn't there.

# Chapter 40

IT DIDN'T MAKE SENSE. I mean I suppose it did — he was free to spend time anywhere he wanted. A hotel, with one of his girls, he could be anywhere. But...

Something just nagged at me.

I shook it off and got busy checking everything I could. And yeah, that included under the bed.

I did a quick sweep of the bedroom and there was nothing more than clothes and a bed.

In the office, a rather ornate cherry wood desk sat in the corner like mine so he could face the door. It had only one drawer in it; that ran the full length of it. There was nothing more than paper, pencils, and one fountain pen with ink. I looked further back into it and did find a small .25 pearl handled automatic.

Pearl handles were for women.

A couple of cabinets against the wall had a few books, none of them read from the looks of it. I stepped back and looked at everything and realized it was all for show. Like the house itself.

I honestly wondered if he even lived here.

I was getting frustrated.

A quick check of the living room and the kitchen revealed

nothing else, then I realized there was one place I hadn't checked. The garage.

There were simple, dark garage doors in the front that matched the shutters around the place. Have to keep up the theme, I guessed. But there was also a small side door with a pane of glass to look in. I looked in, and there was nothing. In other words, no bed.

I opened the small door and walked inside. It was dark and the smell of gasoline and oil was over everything. The light shone in from the open door but I found a switch and threw it. A small bare bulb came on above me and I could at least see around.

There was a small, dark work bench at the end of the garage, a few dusty tools scattered along its top. Beneath was a shelf with one old and rusted gasoline can sitting on it.

There wasn't even a rake in the place. But there were two things on the floor.

The black thing was a small puddle of oil, with the center showing fresh drops of oil. He did make it a habit of being home. And the white thing — was a small slip of paper.

I picked up the paper and walked to the door and into the light of the outside. The paper had an address on it, a street, and numbers.

The street — Wilshire.

The numbers — Millie's apartment building.

Then I ran.

# Chapter 41

I WAS ON WILSHIRE, flying toward Millie's. At least as fast as I could without getting pulled over. Me wanted for murder and all.

I had run back into Carlo's house from the garage and called the Viceroy just to make sure. Mother said Millie hadn't come into work this morning, which was what I was afraid of. And expected.

I don't know how Carlo knew about Millie. Probably had me watched.

A truck cut in front of me just past Rampart and I swerved into oncoming traffic.

Horns exploded all around me and I jerked the wheel back just in time to get out of the way of the Cadillac coming toward me — and cut off the son of a bitch truck that cut me off in the first place.

I heard him hit his brakes, then a crash from somewhere behind me and I assumed, right into the back of him.

Good.

Only a little farther I hit Millie's building and pulled up in front.

I raced up the walk and into the front door, right under her apartment.

I got to the second floor and tried to calm myself as I walked up the wooden floor of the roomy hall until I got to the door in the middle of the hall, right about where the front door would open out below.

I knocked on the door and tried not to ram it in. I didn't need anyone seeing me here in case there was something on the other side of the door that I didn't want to see. I was already up for one murder, probably six, but I was smart and didn't want to make it more.

I knocked a couple more times, maybe a little too hard, then when nothing happened, I pulled out my picks and bent down to the door to—

And a door opened behind me.

A woman about fifty stood there, her white apron over a dark blue dress. She wore sensible shoes and held a young baby on her hip. The baby was dressed in pink. "Can I help you?" She didn't sound too helpful.

I got up, a little embarrassed. "I'm looking for Millie."

"Yeah, you look like it." She looked me up and down, probably ready to call the cops. "You look like one of her customers."

I didn't say anything.

"Yeah, I know what she does." She reached over to smooth the baby's hair, letting her know everything was all right.

"Look, I'm actually a PI. And I do know her. She didn't show up for work today and I'm a little worried."

"And you thought you'd go in to see if she was there?"

I took a deep breath. "It's the only thing I can think to do. I'm worried."

The woman had a long face, with thin cheeks that dropped like they had given up. "Well, you're not going to find her in there."

"Why?"

"About five this morning, I heard voices outside my door. When I opened the door to check to see what the racket was all about, there was two guys with her down at the end of the hall, just shuffling her into the elevator. They seemed to be having a problem with her. She looked like she was drunk."

She wasn't drunk. They'd probably hit her. By the time I got her home she was sober. Or at least near enough to it that she could bust my chops.

"What'd they look like?"

"They were about the same height, short. About my height."

She was five-six.

"One was thinner than the other. The bigger one, he looked all hairy, like he hadn't shaved in a couple days. But his head was almost bald."

It was Carlo and Vince.

I headed for the elevator myself.

The woman called out from behind me. "What do you want me to do with her?"

I stopped and turned around. "What?"

The woman nodded at the baby. "The girl. What do you want me to do with her? I can't watch her all day, you know. I only do it as a favor."

"She's *Millie's*?"

The woman nodded. "Shocked me, too, when she came up with her. Never knew she had a kid. When she never came home last night, I figured she was working."

I didn't tell the woman Millie was with me.

She looked down at the little girl. "So I kept her. What was I gonna do? Throw her out? Then the commotion last night. She in any trouble, Millie?"

"Maybe." Hell yes, she was. I headed to the stairs next to the elevator. They would be faster.

The woman shouted after me. "So what am I supposed to do with her? I got my own life to live, you know?"

I didn't answer.

I hit the stairs and didn't stop.

That kid wasn't going to lose her mother.

# Chapter 42

I WALKED INTO THE Santorini and the guy behind the counter smiled. Actually smiled at me.

"Where's Carlo?"

The guy kept smiling as he walked out from behind the counter. He was big, six-four big, with shoulders the size of a freighter and arms the size of oaks. They stretched his brown and white striped shirt. "You should be in jail." He grinned even more.

I guess Carlo didn't keep secrets too well. "Are you going to tell me or am I going to have to beat it out of you?" He kept coming at me, so I pulled a gun.

I never expected him to be so fast.

He reached out with a fist and slapped at the gun, and it went flying down the hall. Of course that was just after it fired, just missing the guy, and hitting a wall on the other side of him. I hoped there wasn't somebody having fun on the other side of it.

The guy's hand clamped down on my wrist and he wrenched it. That didn't feel so good so I kneed him in the crotch to get his attention. It did. Then he looked at me, just in time to see my fist come into his face.

I slammed him hard but he didn't drop. Then he took a swing

at me and connected. I did drop.

Black swam at the edges of my vision.

He walked down the hall to get my gun. It was ten feet away.

When he got halfway there, the black finally started to creep back out. Then I pulled my other gun and ran to him. Funny enough, I was quiet.

As he bent down to pick up the gun, my other gun crashed into his head and he did drop. Finally. That's why I carry a .45, they had a lot of weight. There wasn't much you could do with a .38 but shoot it, and what's the fun of that when you didn't exactly need to kill someone, just drop 'em to sleep for a bit.

The guy obliged, completely out, and I dragged him back behind the counter. Then I ripped out the telephone line from the wall and tied him with it. Jim could afford to get a new telephone. I was rather partial to my life.

One guy down, and a telephone out of commission. All in all, good so far. Now I had to find Carlo, although with the gunshot, my guess was he already knew I was there.

I walked over to pick up my first gun, just as a bunch of johns poked their heads from the top of the stairs. I guess to see if the shooting had stopped. "It's all right, come on down. We were just having a little party."

They looked from me to the set of shoes poking out from behind the counter. A pair of size twelve brown ones, complete with a hole in the right sole and a piece of cardboard covering it up from the inside.

All the Johns shot down the stairs fast and kept on running.

I kept thinking of my reading lessons.

*See Dick run.*

Then I ran up the stairs against them.

At the second floor, most of the doors were open with a couple still closed, including Carlo's.

Since I wasn't already dead after the racket I caused downstairs, I assumed Carlo wasn't in the place. He or Vince would have been down right away and most likely plugged me from the stairs. Guy from the counter around me or not. But I couldn't take any chances.

I pressed myself against the wall on the far side from the door handle into his room, twisted it, and flung the door in hard.

Nothing. No gunshot came as a "Welcome home, love."

Even so, I got down low and poked my head in. Nothing. The room was empty except for the table, the two chairs, and the golden light trying to push out the stale cigarette smoke that hung in the air. A couple of mangled, dead butts were in the ashtray on the table. Other than that, Carlo and Vince weren't around. Which meant they weren't here to begin with. They were probably with Millie, and I had a bad feeling about where they took her.

I ducked into the room to see if there was anything else of use, like an address of a torture house, but there was nothing.

I slipped back out into the hall and everything was quiet.

Light streamed into the hall from all the open doors. All the doors but one. Eula's door next door. Still closed.

I did the same routine, pressing myself against the wall farthest from the doorknob. Maybe Carlo was in here, maybe Vince was, too. Maybe I'd find Millie in here. I hoped I didn't. I guess I figured if I found her, it may not be the way I wanted. I twisted the knob and shoved the door in.

There was only a cry as the door slammed to the other side, then a soft whimpering, low and odd, like it was well-practiced.

I led with one gun and looked around the doorway. In the corner was a girl in an ivory-colored slip, curled up into the best approximation of a ball I had ever seen. Tight-wound, her head tucked into her lap, her whimpering and sniffling smothered themselves into the tops of her thighs.

I looked left and then right in the room and decided it was empty, except for the girl in the corner.

Eula.

I walked in sideways, keeping an eye, and one gun, on the door. The others I kept on Eula but I guessed I wouldn't need it. I squatted next to her. "It's okay, Eula. It's all over."

Curled up in the corner, her reaction seemed a little more

than I would expect from one gunshot and a little bit of fighting coming from downstairs. But who was I?

Then I saw the old and nearly faded bruises on her thighs. Not the deep ones that the girls in the pics had. These were random, and given often. I knew those kinds.

And I thought of my mother.

Looking at Eula curled in the corner reminded me of her. I guess corners provided at least some kind of protection when you were used to none at all.

It ripped at me, and after the fun downstairs, I started to feel that deep-seated anger rise up in me again. I holstered the one gun I had on her. "It's okay, no one is going to come for you. I'm here now."

The crying continued for a bit and I had enough sense not to touch her. She only met me the one time, didn't know me. The only thing that would do would be to trigger her.

I wondered what was happening to Millie right now. I tried not to think about that. Well, I did, to keep my focus up. "Listen, I have a problem."

I wanted to find out anything I could, but I really didn't have a lot of time. With them taking Millie, I knew they wouldn't be keeping her around for a while. If they picked her up, it was because they thought she knew something. And she did. About the black-and-blue parties. At least how they started. And by who.

I kept my voice smooth, and quiet. "Listen, they took someone. I'm not sure if you know Millie — bottle-blonde hair, she works up at the Viceroy downtown. You know her?"

No reaction but the crying died down.

I kept up with my patter. "Well, I've known her a bit. Remember, Jim Nolan asked me to find out who has been... hurting the girls."

A deep sob from the curled-up mass of flesh and bruises cried out.

I don't care how many people you've killed in war, how many people you've hurt — when a young girl is lying inches away from you, you want to help. And I was doing the best I could.

"Well, he wants to protect you." Okay, it was a bit of a stretch, he only really wanted to protect the business.

But I wanted to protect them.

I looked at Eula's bruises and I realized where I was, the room right next to Carlo's. I remembered the old man, and how he wouldn't let go of my mother, wouldn't let her out of his sight. How he needed to know where she was almost all the time.

"I'm pretty sure it was Carlo who killed all the girls. But he's not going to bother you anymore. I promise."

Another round of sobs released from Eula but she sounded like she was almost out of steam. I heard actual breathing between the sobs.

"You'll never have to worry again. I promise. I'll stop him. Permanently. I promise."

"And… Vince?" The question came out muffled, and haltingly, but there was a measure of hate in there.

Maybe I had a chance.

"Him, too."

I watched as Eula's small, exposed shoulders let go just a bit. Her head was still balled up inside her, but there was a loosening.

The sobs had stopped and only a few sniffles remained as first one leg, then the other, explored the empty space around them, stretching out just a bit to make sure there was room. There was. I backed off and made sure of it.

I pulled a white handkerchief out of my jacket pocket and extended it to her.

She took it.

She relaxed and came up to sitting in the crook of the corner, the golden light playing halfway down her light brown hair. It was stringy and stuck out in places.

"I need to ask you some questions."

Eula looked up at me, her brown eyes catching light from the window and actually looking lighter. "All right."

Her breathing was still ragged, her eyes looked like they wanted to bolt, but God help her, she stayed there.

I took out the pics of the girls getting hit.
She sat there, coldness creeping back into her eyes.
Then she told me what I wanted to know.

# Chapter 43

THE HOUSE WAS IN Signal Hill.

And I was heading to it, fast.

Seems the wall between Eula's room and Carlo's was thin, and she could hear everything he and Vince said. I'm sure she used it to keep on his good side. When you were a possession, you needed to know which way the wind was blowing each day.

Eula told me what she had heard through the wall and it wasn't much. But it was everything.

She told me Carlo would talk to Vince about having someone over for a "party." Exactly the term Millie had used. His beating nights. His black-and-blue parties.

According to her, he kept mentioning the hill when he talked about the house. *I'll head out to the hill. . . I'll get things ready at the hill.* She didn't know where that was and it could have been anywhere. There were the hills that ran between Los Angeles and the San Fernando Valley to the north. There were hills further out to the east, there were the hills that looked out over Malibu and north, and there were hills that ran inland and to the south.

But then she mentioned one other thing: oil.

They'd also talk about the hill house and how much oil was

163

pumping, the expiration of a lease — all sorts of things that Eula knew nothing about but as she told them to me, that little area in the back of my head started wondering something. Maybe the hill was actually the Hill, and there was only one hill in all of Los Angeles that had oil everywhere on it — Signal Hill.

Located just south of Los Angeles and right next to Long Beach, Signal Hill had another name that most people knew it by, Porcupine Hill, because there were so many oil derricks sticking out of the place. Literally hundreds and hundreds of them.

Once oil was discovered around Los Angeles in the very late 1800s, the number of wells shot from eighty to over five hundred in just three years. Then the '20s hit and it was a free-for-all.

Now large parts of Los Angeles were covered in oil derricks. A black, thick-smelling forest of derricks that runs right up to the ocean in places. And in this case, all over Signal Hill.

As soon as I left the Santorini, I headed straight for the Signal Hill city offices. Every city has bureaucracy. And if there's anything I know, especially in LA, where there's bureaucracy there's someone looking to make a buck.

It took only fifteen minutes, and twenty bucks, to get the addresses of a series of houses owned by one Carlo Genovese at the edge of Signal Hill. From what I knew, most of the oil up on the hill itself was taken over by the larger companies, companies that kept a lot of Los Angeles' men, and families, rich.

But at the outskirts, at the rough edges of the city, was more of a free-for-all where derricks were mixed with houses. Black-timbered derricks crowding behind, in front of, and pushing out the houses.

The sun had already set by the time I got to the neighborhood.

The hillside was somewhat steep and there weren't a lot of houses left. But there were derricks poking up and out of the ground everywhere, like skeleton trees, made of black and heavy wooden timbers, they knifed the darkening sky as if defying anything natural from being there.

The clangs and bangs were harsh and relentless from the

pumps, beating out hard mechanical heartbeats the same as the engines that consumed what they brought to the surface. The smell was heavy, and dark, smothering as only thick raw crude can be.

Driving through it was as if all the life had been sucked out of the area, the few old and grayed clapboard homes left, a testament to all the life that used to be here. Lives long gone now.

Except a home for black-and-blue parties.

I got to the street that the woman in the registrar's office gave me, right at the edge of the city and the edge of the hill. Past a forest of dark derricks holding close to the hill was a cluster of three houses. The only ones remaining in the area. And two cars.

They were there. And if I didn't miss my guess, that was Carlo, Vince, and the goon they'd sent to the warehouse for me. Three against one, I could live with that.

I drove up the road that ran below the houses, pulled up next to one of the derricks a little ways away from the houses, and got out. And I pulled both my guns.

A light shone in the first house, yellow slivers of it poking out from behind three first-floor windows. Two windows on the side and one in the front. The shades were drawn. There was nothing from the other two houses.

The first house was a two-story clapboard like the rest that I'd passed on the way in. It was raised up off the road on the hill, a small wall in front of the house like a terrace, meant to stop it from falling down, I guessed.

There were a line of derricks in back of the three houses, a couple in front, and a group of three on the side of the house that I was now facing.

As I walked closer, another light caught my eye close to the ground, at the base of the house. Another sliver, a brighter one, came from the edges of a small rectangular window down there. The basement.

I walked up the small hill to the house, then worked my way to the basement window. Cardboard was stuffed into the thing so I couldn't see anything on the other side, except the hint of bright light that came from its edges. And Jolson. Someone was playing music to hit by. That is, if they were hitting her, and I hoped they were, because that meant she was still alive.

I did a quick circle of the place and found a set of weathered gray storm doors leading down into the basement on the other side of the house. There were also front and back doors, but those were less desirable; walking over the wood floor of a house that had probably stood here for at least the past thirty years was not the best of ideas. I had had plenty of practice sneaking around on a creaking wooden floor I knew, I did not want to be walking on one I didn't.

So I went back to the basement storm doors.

I couldn't hear the music from this side, and there was no light coming from the one window that looked down at the base of the house.

I walked quietly to the gray wooden doors that slanted down and led to the basement below. Slipping one gun back into its holster, I pulled gently at the worn wooden handle nailed to one of the doors. The door pulled up half an inch and then stopped. I could see the glint of a steel padlock on the other side. Locked from the inside. They definitely didn't want anyone coming down unannounced.

Then I heard another door creak open from the other side.

I set the door back, and with nowhere to go, flattened myself against the house.

I heard the distinctive click as the padlock below was opened.

The wooden door opposite me pushed up, creaking into the clanging night. Then it was followed by a hand, and that was followed by — Vince.

The door slapped down carelessly on the other side from me and Vince walked up and out of the basement facing forward, looking into the blackness of the night. At least he was alone. He reached for something in his coat, then pulled out a pack of cigarettes. He pulled one out with his lips, then struck a match, all the while looking forward.

Then his shoulders tensed and he froze. Then a slight twitch in the edge of his right shoulder told me he was reaching for something.

I couldn't risk a gunshot, either from him or me, so I stepped quickly onto the closed door in front of me, planted the other foot on the edge of the frame, and launched myself right as Vince spun around.

I caught the silver glint of a gun coming out of his coat, then hit him square in the chest with all six feet of ex-Marine, taking him to the ground with me.

I felt his gun underneath me and quickly got hold of it and his hand. We kept everything silent, almost, two guys just rolling and hitting as best we could, to the background clangs of the machinery in the night.

I finally landed a clear fist into Vince's mug. That loosened things for a bit, then I ripped the gun out of his hand and tossed it over the edge of the front of the house. It hit the road below, far enough away.

I reached for my guns, just as another glint of silver lashed out from Vince, a knife. I held up both arms to block it, rolling back at the same time.

I didn't want to shoot, to alert Carlo and whoever else was in there; the only thing I had at the moment was surprise and that was quickly fading away.

I felt something nick my right shoulder, then I twisted around and lashed out with my foot. I caught him square in the wrist and I heard bones snap. The knife went flying over the edge like the gun, then like a cat with nine lives, Vince came up with another knife.

I reached out quick with one gun and caught him in the face. Dazed, he stepped back and I saw my chance. I charged him.

It was a stupid move because basically, the only thing in back of him was air, and the drop down to the road below. Being smart was never one of my strong suits, but taking advantage of an opening was.

I caught him in the gut and wrapped my arms around his

back, hoping I'd at least land on him instead of on my head, or onto his knife.

We landed with a sickening crunch, me rolling over him and flat out onto the road. I was dazed, but fought off the twirling in my head, trying to get a bead on him with my guns to convince him to stay down. I didn't have to worry.

Vince lay on the ground, his head at a completely unnatural angle.

As in broken.

Well not his head, his neck. And he didn't move.

I checked him and he was dead. One down.

One or two to go.

# Chapter 44

I WALKED DOWN THE storm door stairs, both guns drawn.

The lights were completely off in the basement but I heard the music coming from further inside. It was an up-tempo jazz tune now, complete with saxes and trumpets wailing, but beyond that I heard the hits.

Soft, meaty thuds, tinged with the slight snap of skin to skin. Immediately my whole body started to buzz, electricity flowing through it, my breathing shutting off and that old, familiar taste of bile coming up my throat. Like when I was a kid.

I searched around for a door, but the only thing I could make out was a large camera on a tripod, its lens pressed against the wall.

The music wound up to a trombone solo, the slide of the notes up and down the scale, punctuated by blasted wails, as if it was singing straight from hell.

I remembered one time, the old man got going on my mother when I was young, and to cover her screams he ran the sound up on the phonograph. I was back there now, but now in a basement, looking to get on the other side of a wall to kill Carlo.

The trombone slipped into drums, the beat matching the slamming of my heart wanting to get out.

I looked into the camera.

It was the room.

I knew it would be.

Millie lay on the bed, naked, tied at all four corners, and over her stood the tall bald guy, his bald head almost touching the ceiling, and his fist coming down and driving into her shoulder with a violence I hadn't seen in a long while.

White exploded in my eyes and I couldn't see a thing.

But then I could. It was rage.

Time slowed to clarity, all my senses alert, all my rage rising. I felt like I was guided.

I had rehearsed exactly this, for days, for months, as I went through basic training and then was shipped to France.

As I stalked Germans, as I charged from the lines, as I walked into shattered building after shattered building, I rehearsed exactly this.

In the corner of the room, near where I came in, was an old black changing screen propped against the wall. I walked to it, pulled it back, and there was a door behind it.

I was numb.

I reached for the knob, pulled it back, and had my guns up before the door cleared the front of my face.

I knew Carlo had to be in there, too, and maybe the big guy from the warehouse to watch his back. Or maybe he was upstairs. It didn't matter. I kept inside the dark room, my guns leveled at the tall bald guy across the bed.

As the door opened, he flashed his face up at me, the sweat falling into his eyes. Eyes that went wide at the sight of the guns. Like he'd seen a ghost.

It was exactly as I planned it. Exactly as I had rehearsed. And I unloaded one clip. Seven rounds, plus one in the chamber, until the slide locked back on the gun, empty, the small barrel of the .45 exposed with nothing more to shoot. At least in that gun.

But I had the other.

I got down low and pushed myself out, my other gun trained

down the side of the wall. Nobody.

Carlo was nowhere.

I looked over and the tall bald guy still stood against the wall, wild and stunned, eight bullet holes surrounding the wall behind him.

I didn't want to kill him. Just get the bastard's attention.

The eight gunshots still hung ringing in the air, the smoke clouding things.

I just wanted to leave him properly scared. I'd deal with him later.

I kept my other gun pointed down the length of the wall. The room was the end of the long length of the basement, the rest of it open but for a set of open stairs leading up at the other end.

Carlo must have headed up them. We didn't have much time.

I looked and Millie's eyes were raging. Screams were probably coming out of her mouth but with the gag it was nothing I could understand.

I pointed my gun at the tall bald guy just to let him know I hadn't forgotten about him. He stood pinned to the wall, the fear of God in his eyes.

I quickly untied one of Millie's hands.

She pulled out the white cloth gag and whispered hoarse. "He's in there — Carlo!"

I followed the line of her hand and it pointed to a closed door just before the stairs. It might be back into the room I'd just come out of, but that room was shorter. Carlo was in another, smaller room.

I pointed my gun at the tall bald guy. "You, stay put."

Millie scrambled to untie her other hand as I holstered my empty gun and pointed the full one toward the closed door at the other end of the basement. And I headed toward it, ready to take on Carlo.

"Hey!" Millie shouted.

I turned, just in time to see the tall bald guy leaping across the bed and out the door next to it. He was gone.

One shot blasted out of the closed door next to me and I ducked back.

The door itself was dark wood and looked sturdy. But not sturdy enough to stop a bullet.

Or my foot.

I kicked it in and backed away fast as four more quick shots came out at me.

Only one of them hit. My shoulder.

The flashes of the gun came from the back left corner of the room, so I leaned in fast and pumped five shots back into it. Nothing else came back at me so I figured I might have hit something.

I looked up and Millie looked back at me from the bed. I waved at her to get the hell out of there, and pointed to the door the tall bald guy had just gone out.

She wrapped a white sheet around her, and went.

"Carlo?"

No answer from inside the small room.

I could hope he was dead — that was my strong hope anyway. If the big guy was upstairs, I still had three shots left. That would have to do me. So I kept my gun moving between the open door to the small room and up the stairs, which was hell because I was shot in my right shoulder.

On second thought, maybe it was only a graze. Otherwise I wouldn't even be able to hold the gun. Well, my night was looking up, wasn't it.

"Carlo! Why don't you come out and we can talk about this."

I saw a half-gallon can of paint under the stairs. I crawled over to it. It felt about half full when I picked it up and thought what the hell, it couldn't hurt.

"Really, just talk."

I pulled myself back across the basement floor until I was at the door again. There was no sound from inside. Like I could even hear it after all the shots in that basement. The ringing in my ears continued like I'd been caught in the middle of a church bell.

I adjusted myself so that I was just near the opening of the door. I set my gun down on the floor in front of me, grabbed the handle of the paint can, and flung it into the back corner.

A single shot exploded from inside the room and the door jamb opposite me splintered.

That was six shots. The only question was, did Carlo have a revolver or an automatic? He was either empty or had a couple more left.

I looked up the stairs and still nobody had come down, which was good. Either the big guy from the warehouse was never here, or he'd already run. I liked that either way.

"Carlo?"

"What?" Alive. But he sounded weak.

Keeping behind the door where I was, I looked through the doorway into the small room.

I adjusted myself. My shoulder hurt like hell. "One thing I could never understand, why did you cut them up? I mean, why not just get rid of the bodies?"

A small laugh and a cough sounded from the other side of the doorway. "Ah... can't take credit for that one, Devin. I just took lemons, and made money off them."

"What the hell does that mean?"

"Someone else did the other girls. I just followed them... figured why not, use it. Pile a few more on and let whoever did it take the fall for all of them."

I began to hear his breathing; it wasn't good.

"That bald son of a bitch out there — I hope you got him, by the way — he's what started it. He was working on a girl and bam, she up and dies on us. Right there in the bed. Surprised the hell out of us."

"So you cut her up, too?"

He laughed again. "No, he did. He wanted to."

"He do all of your girls?"

"Hell, yeah." There was a smile in Carlo's voice. "And he paid for them all."

"You know who did the others?"

"No. And I don't care."

"Just so I know, because I'm keeping track, Carlo — which ones did you do?"

"Who cares — Helen, Holly, and Patty."

That was the name of the dark curls — Patty.

"And the others?"

"Not mine."

I heard something back by the other door and Millie, wrapped in her sheet, walked back in. Backwards, followed by the big guy from the warehouse.

He was as huge as he was in the warehouse, even bigger, his black hat still on the top of his head.

And he held Vince's nickel-plated gun — pointing right at Millie's head.

# Chapter 45

THERE I WAS, LYING on the basement floor, three bullets left to my name, and now the big guy from the warehouse showed up, Vince's gun pointed at Millie's head.

The night just kept getting better.

I swung my gun over at the big guy.

Then he pulled Millie in front of him, the gun still at her head. He looked at me, a question on his face. "You killed Vince?"

He still sounded simple, but his powers of observation were astounding.

I kept my gun pointed at the big guy since Carlo was buried back in the back of the other room.

Just once I wished for a clean shot out in the open.

"Did you kill Vince?"

"You already asked me that."

"Did you kill Vince?"

He had a one track mind. "Well, it may have been the fall but to be honest with you, I did kind of feel his neck snap when I landed on him."

It took the big guy a little to work through that, I guess working out all the logistics in his head of what I just said.

"Sonny... Mr. Devin is all right. He saved me."

Sonny? The big guy's name was Sonny? I supposed it fit, in a stuck-in-his-childhood kind of way.

"Sonny, please take the gun away from my head."

Sonny didn't listen. He just kept focused on me. "Did you kill Carlo, too?"

I nodded in toward the room on the other side of me. "Well, he was talking as of a little bit ago, so no. Not yet. But I pumped a few shots into there and from the sounds of him, he's not doing so good."

That seemed to brighten Sonny.

Sonny walked Millie toward me and the open doorway. "Sonny, you know, let Millie stay back there. She's not going to do anything to you, are you Millie?"

Millie looked back at Sonny. "Sonny, you know me..."

I wished I knew who the hell he was.

"...I promise. I'm not going to do anything."

Sonny looked like he was trying to work through what he was supposed to do. This was going to take all night. "Sonny."

He looked down at me, his mouth twitching, but Vince's gun still pointed at Millie's head.

"Sonny, look, she promised. She's not going to do anything to you. And I promise, too." Okay, that was a lie, but there was something about him that I just did not understand. And he definitely didn't fit in with the goons that Carlo normally hired. If he was one of them, Millie and I would both be dead by now. But I'm a survivor, and I was definitely not going to let him do anything to Millie and hopefully, not to me. "Let her go."

And Sonny did.

I nodded Millie away and she headed to the other side of the room but stayed inside, near the bed. I wanted her to get out of there completely, one less thing to worry about, but she was stubborn.

I kept my gun on Sonny, but nodded to him. "You did good." I don't know why I said that but it felt like the right thing to do.

Like a kid needing to be stroked

Sonny swung the gun to the open doorway. "Carlo is in there?"

"Yeah, but—"

Sonny walked right into the doorway.

I yelled. "Sonny!" but it was too late.

Two shots rang out from inside the room and Sonny shuddered both times, but then he opened up with the nickeled gun and emptied the thing into the far corner of the room.

Then he fell against the wall, then crept down it, the two bullet holes in his gut starting to bloom red with blood.

He fell to the floor in front of me, across the opening of the door. I quickly flashed my face in the doorway, then pulled it back. No other shots came from inside. I hoped that meant Carlo was dead.

I flashed my face in a couple more times with no response, then walked into the room with my gun pointed forward. It wasn't needed. Carlo lay in the corner of the room, propped up, his back against the corner but head hanging down, as if looking at the six shots he took in the rest of his body.

I kicked the gun away from him and it slid across the concrete floor, trailing his blood behind.

Millie hung over Sonny, the sheet covering her dropping half down onto him. "What were you doing here?"

Sonny's eyes were open and in shock. "I didn't want to kill you."

He said this to Millie. Millie looked up at me.

"Ma wanted me to, but I didn't want to." Then he looked up at me. "Is Carlo dead?"

I nodded to him. "Yeah. You got him." I wasn't sure why that felt right to say, too.

"Good." Sonny tried a smile and actually got a bit of a one. "Ma'll be happy."

I lowered my voice to Millie. "Who's Ma?"

"Mother Angela."

He was Mother Angela's son?

Sonny looked up at Millie, looking into her face. "Ma wanted me to kill you. But I wouldn't." Then he looked at me. "Wanted me to kill you, too, after you wouldn't listen. But I figured I'd kill Carlo first, because you'd already killed Vince. Ma said Vince was dangerous."

I nodded. Then looked down at his hand. He still held Vince's gun. I knelt down and pulled it away from him. Just in case.

Millie loosened his shirt. It wouldn't be doing him any good. "Why did you want to kill me?"

Sonny nodded toward me. "Because you was talkin' with him."

I figured one question wouldn't hurt. "Did you kill the girls, Sonny?"

"Yep. All three of them. Plus one I tried to, but she bit me. I didn't kill her."

Eula.

Then he winced. The shock was wearing off. I'd seen a lot of guys die in my day, and any of them gut-shot died fast. It opened everything inside you. And you didn't have a chance.

"Tell Ma I killed Carlo, Millie. She'll be happy."

Then his eyes shut and he was still.

Millie looked up at me, a lot of confusion in her eyes, but for me, a lot more things started making sense. About as much sense as could be made of all of this.

Then Millie stood up quickly. "I have to get back to my place."

I thought of the little girl with the woman across the hall. "I saw her. You didn't tell me you had a kid."

She looked at me, starting to cry. "She's not mine, she's Holly's."

"Holly's?"

Millie nodded, I think the weight of everything finally hitting her. "I watched her whenever Holly would…" She looked at the bed at the other end of the room, "…come here, I guess." Then she looked back at me. "She was saving up so she could take Millicent away. She worked nights, so I was always able to watch her."

I didn't think they were that close. "How long did you know her?"

"I found her in an automat, three years ago." More tears came. "I told her about working… if she wanted to make a buck."

And that was it. The tears let loose and came hot and hard for Millie.

A river of them.

# Chapter 46

I CALLED CARDON AFTER that from a phone upstairs, after I had cleaned the place of anything that might have led back to Jim. There wasn't much, except the ledger that Carlo kept in the house. Just like Rose's ledger at the Pacific Surf. Just like all the records that all the hotels kept.

I moved it out to Bella's car and stuffed it under the back seat.

Millie called her neighbor to let her know that she would be coming home, well, soon. But soon didn't completely describe it.

Cardon made it over in half an hour, followed by the DA's boys and the coroner. I'd rather have not been there, and I definitely didn't want Millie there, but seeing as how I was currently up for six murders — well, seven with the latest girl Cardon found this morning — it seemed the only way I was going to avoid a trial. And the noose waiting at the end of it.

So we sat there like nice little kids and told the men exactly what had happened.

It also helped that another used saw was found in the basement. Plus a hose and drain in the little room that Carlo ended up in, with enough evidence still left in it to prove what had happened in there.

I was honest, and told Cardon that he'd find a few of my bullets in Carlo. But after pointing out the important fact that Carlo was tossing them at me to begin with, I convinced Cardon to state that very important fact in his report. A report that would close the case on the murders of the six prostitutes, with Carlo, Vince, and Sonny sharing equal billing.

Although they didn't know Sonny's name. On account of the fact that I had taken his wallet and stuffed it in Bella's back seat, too. And taken his car, and driven it a ways away and had Millie follow in Bella's car to drive us both back to the house.

That's when I called Cardon.

If they found Sonny's name, they'd find Mother Angela; and if they found her, that might open up a whole lot of canned worms for Jim.

And if there's anything that Jim hated, it was attention.

So after we finished at the house, two hours after midnight, I took Millie home, and then kept driving.

I had to go to the Viceroy.

And deal with Mother Angela.

Whatever that was going to be.

# Chapter 47

I WALKED INTO THE Viceroy like I did the first time, but in the middle of the night, the place was dead. Surprisingly dead.

A light shone from the end of the hall, down near the kitchen, so I headed for it. I didn't realize before, but Mother Angela actually lived at the hotel. Millie told me. Sonny lived there too. I guess Rose did at her hotel.

I just wanted an answer. I had Carlo's answer, why they killed the girls they killed: for money. But Mother Angela? It made no sense.

Ruthie, Ellie, Dorthia... and maybe the latest one that Cardon told me about, found this morning. I had no idea who she even was. Carlo didn't say anything about any new one, so it was probably Sonny there, too.

I got to the door at the end of the corridor and Mother sat inside a room similar to Rose's. A desk, a chair, and a filing cabinet. An empty, barren, sad room, and Mother sat at the desk.

My final step at the open door hit a creak in the floorboard.

Mother turned. "Why are you so..." She stopped as she saw me. "...late." Her mouth stayed open a bit. Then she shut it.

Her one crazy eye searched me, then I saw her searching in her own mind as to what it meant, me alive. So I told her. "Sonny's dead."

Then, as she sat there, it looked like her entire world deflated. No, not deflated, died.

Her ledger lay open behind her, on the desk, and a small open cigar box sat next to it with all the singles and fives that young and old men alike had left today for a turn at their version of fun.

I thought of the girls, of Holly's photo, of her mother, of Millie... and Millicent. None of this made any sense. None of it. "Why?"

"Why, what?" Her voice was mostly calm, with a hint of resignation in it.

"You told Sonny to kill the girls?"

Her expression didn't change, but her eyes did. They became detached. "Yeah."

Maybe she was detached... from her head. I couldn't believe it, it was that simple to her — *yeah*. "But why?"

Mother pulled out a broken cigarette from her skirt and lit it. "You wouldn't understand."

I got mad. "Try me."

Mother held her finger hooked over the cigarette, still like a hawk. "Sonny and me started a diner. Saved everything we had, working at this place — twelve years, cooking for these... women." She looked up at whatever lay above her, disgust in her face. "Listening to it all day long."

I didn't hear a thing.

Then she looked back at me. "You know they'll open their legs for anything."

"You didn't have to work here."

Her look dropped to hate. "I just wanted to leave."

"To open a diner."

"To open my *dream*." Her cigarette was about crushed. But she kept going. "You ever have a business, Devin?"

"Every day."

"Right — you're a PI — lucky you — well, me and Sonny

had saved up—"

"You said that already."

"Don't," her blue eyes went to ice, "interrupt." I think if she'd had a gun she would have shot me then and there. "We rented a place over on Fifth. It had a griddle and counter but the rest of it was a wreck. We took three weeks to clean, paint, Sonny repaired everything in sight, and right at the end we brought in new tables and chairs. Red ones. Special bought. So we could make it up just like what I had in my dreams. And you know what happened?"

"Someone broke up the place."

"No — *Carlo* broke up the place. And that silent bastard of his, Vince. We walked up to open it our first day, we walked up to the back door and it was already open, and I knew something bad had happened. I couldn't just have my dream. No. Couldn't. Ever. So we walked inside and everything in the kitchen area was on the floor — the eggs, flour, milk, salt, a whole side of beef, everything. Just thrown around like they were kids havin' a ball. Then outside in the diner…" She stopped, her eyes gone inward, looking at a scene only she could see for herself. "My furniture — every last stick of chair, every goddamn table — everything, broken up and laying in red pieces on the floor."

And to Mother Angela, killing the girls, was just furniture being broken to her.

"And you know what — you know what, I told him, I told Carlo five months before we were leaving, and he didn't look for someone to replace us. Never. I kept asking him, 'when are you going to bring someone in?' And he'd look at me all smug and say it would all be handled. All along, he knew what he was going to do. They wouldn't let us leave." She looked down at the near-finished cigarette in her hand. "They wouldn't let us leave. So after they broke up the diner, we had nothing. And we came back here. They wouldn't let us leave."

I'm not sure how much Jim had to do with this, but my guess was not a lot. He was a businessman — and like the girls, whenever you needed someone new, you just brought in someone else. Knowing Carlo, it was probably all him. A possessive bastard to the core.

A muffled thumping started up from the room above us. Apparently the place never rested.

Mother Angela looked up, then with a look of utter disgust, nodded back toward the ledger in back of her. "I added it up for six months, and found out who was the top earner."

"Ruthie?"

"Yeah, Ruthie."

"What about Ellie?"

A short laugh shot out of Mother Angela. "She was just a pain in the ass."

Unbelievable.

There was no justice in any of this. The girls couldn't come back. Mother Angela seemed to have started it all, or... did Carlo? It didn't matter. They all danced their dance and the only one left out of it was Millicent.

The thumping continued above.

I guess life goes on.

I was already in the clear. The cops had Carlo and Vince and Sonny for the murders, so the only thing left to deal with was Mother Angela.

The easiest thing would be to call the cops. Add her to the list of murderers, or at least as an accessory. Which somehow didn't seem like enough.

I think I'd seen enough hate and anger to last a lifetime on this case, and look where it had gotten everyone. Maybe it was good my old man died before I could get to him. Maybe that helped both of us.

I felt the anger, the hate I felt for him, drop away a bit. Not completely, it was always going to be with me, it had to. For what he had done. But maybe it was more the vengeance that had separated away, looking at Mother Angela in the chair in front of me, as broken as a piece of furniture.

You kept emotions out of cases. That was the only way you

could survive in this business. What's done is done, and nothing I can do now will bring back Holly, or any of the other girls. Nothing. Now I just have to clean up the mess.

So instead of calling the cops — they already had enough names for the murders — I called Jim. The cops, coming into the Viceroy, would only open up more problems that didn't need to be opened.

So I called Jim.

"I can't thank you enough, John. You've protected me. And I appreciate it."

It wasn't so much protecting Jim, although it seemed inviting the cops into the Viceroy here would only add more… problems. And I was done with problems for one night. Hell, one lifetime.

And I guess in the end, what went on in this hotel was nothing for me to judge. Hell, even in the beginning it's nothing for me to judge. People decide to do what they want to do in order to keep a roof over their head, and a few meals a day on the table. And I get to choose for myself. It's the only way I could sleep at night. At least, when I could sleep.

And I'm not sure I would for a while. All I could see in my mind were the faces — the dead heads from Bartie's pictures. And Holly was one of them.

And Ruthie.

And Ellie.

And Helen.

And Dorthia.

And… Patty. Patty with the dark curls.

And I guess there was a new one, a seventh. God help her whoever she was.

Seven is not a lucky number.

Jake and Easy showed up quickly; I guess there wasn't much traffic.

They took Mother.

Maybe for a ride to the mountains.

# Chapter 48

MILLIE STOOD ON THE open-air train platform holding Millicent.

I laughed. It was the first time I got the fact that they had the same first name.

Hell of a PI.

Millie wore a dove gray hat, a close-fitting one that actually looked nice on her. Her dress was a deep navy that fell to her knees. All in all, the perfect get-up for a woman heading back to the Midwest. Or… I wasn't sure if Minnesota counted as the Midwest or not.

With a couple of calls I had located Holly's sister out there, and she had agreed to take Millicent in. Millie agreed to take her. She wanted her change. The money from Holly's yellow shoe box was going home with Millicent to give her a start.

Millicent had begun to grow on Millie and I wondered how this was all going to sit with her. Taking her there. But Holly's sister was a blood relative and Millie couldn't deny that.

"All aboard!"

The conductor was up at the head of the train but his voice carried far enough for us to hear it. Millie looked at me, a bit of a smile on her face. Millicent reached up and grabbed at Millie's hat and pulled it off.

The smile on Millicent's face was priceless as she succeeded at something. A big thing for a little girl.

Then she dropped the hat to the platform.

I smiled, then bent and picked it up. I went to hand it to Millie, who looked at me with her hands full... what was she going to do with it?

So she handed Millicent to me, smiling, I think liking the uncomfortable look on my mug, and took back her hat. "You don't mind, do you?" Her smile had something at the edges, like the smirk of a priest handing a two-foot crucifix to a six-foot sinner.

It felt awkward in my hands. I mean the baby. Millicent did. "How are you supposed to hold her?"

Millie laughed as she adjusted her hat. "You're doing just fine."

Millicent reached up and, passing on my brown hat, grabbed my nose instead. The kid had a grip. "Hey..." I reached up and, despite the laughing of Millicent in my arms, a rather too-joyous squeal if you asked me, I managed to pull her hand away from my nose. Then Millicent grabbed onto my big stick of a finger.

And wouldn't let go.

"Hmm..."

Millie opened her purse and took out a cigarette. "Looks like you've made a friend." She lit it and stepped back away from Millicent and me. And Millie just looked at us. Smiling.

I've done some uncomfortable things in my life, but standing there, alone, in the middle of that platform holding a baby, now officially topped the list.

A porter walked past with five bags in his hand, and smiled up at me.

I didn't smile back.

Then a gaggle of women fifteen feet to our left started pointing at me. And smiling.

Yep. Like a sinner holding a crucifix. "You going to hurry up with that cigarette or not?"

Millie kept smiling, and shook her head. "No."

"I'll take back your ticket."

She smiled even bigger. "Then are you going to make the trip?"

Check, and mate.

I looked down, and Millicent had fallen asleep as she still held my finger.

I never looked at a small kid, much less one that was only a little past being a baby. At least up close. Her finger had this tiny little fingernail on it. I didn't think they could get that small. I guess it made sense that she had one. Well actually, ten of them, it's just that… you never really think about something like that.

"You're going to make a good father."

I looked back at Millie and she wasn't laughing. And I was getting less happy by the second. "Are you done yet?"

I felt my two guns beneath my coat, but with Millicent in my arms, I couldn't get to them. I felt like a bull who'd been clipped.

Millie dropped the rest of her cigarette onto the platform and ground it out as the last of the smoke left her red lips. She gently took Millicent back into her arms.

I hoped she'd figure something out in Minnesota. Maybe stay there. Maybe move on to something else.

I bought her the ticket, made it round trip in case she wanted to come back, but inside, I hoped she stayed.

Something different. That was the nice thing about a new city, you could become something different. At least that's what I had done when I stopped in LA — and stayed.

Although I'm not really sure if I became anything different. Maybe I did. Maybe just a little better.

"You're a good man, Devin."

Millie wasn't smiling now. She looked up at me with her green eyes, and they were looking wet.

"Go on, your train's waiting."

Then Millie leaned up to me, Millicent between us, and kissed me light on the cheek. "You take care of yourself."

"You, too. And her." I almost smiled, but didn't.

Two long whistles sounded. "All aboard!"

Millie stepped onto the first step, then made it to the top, then looked back and out.

But not at me. She looked out at Los Angeles, rising up behind us.

Millie stood there for a bit, not moving. I wondered what she was thinking.

Then she just simply turned, walked right into the car, and disappeared. Not looking back once.

Good.

It was a start anyway.

I headed back down the platform as the train pulled out in the opposite direction.

As the cars picked up speed, it made me feel like I was going slower until, with a final blast of air, they were gone and I was left standing on the platform.

Alone.

Which was fine.

I had something to take care of.

All along I'd wanted to stay alone. Was used to it. But I guess I thought of other kids and their families. And how maybe I never really did have one.

I had wanted to kill my old man, and for how long? Every night of my life.

And I never got the chance.

And that ate at me.

But maybe it was a good thing, not killing him. But it had left a big hole in me all these years.

A hole that can pull you down. If you let it. Pull you right down until you can't get out.

I guess the best thing is if you never let yourself down in the hole in the first place.

I showed up at the Trudy a half hour later.

I got out of my car in the fake English courtyard and walked up to the second floor walkway that wobbled and warped, and got myself to number five and knocked.

Charlie answered the door.

I asked him if he wanted to go out for Chinese.

He did. And we did.

# Chapter 49

IT WAS DARK OUTSIDE, black I guess you could say, as I walked down from out of the hills.

The hill itself was steep, the crisp and dry, near-dead brush crackling and catching at my feet and legs as I continued. A full moon shone bright in back of me, on the other side of the hill. But not on this side. Here, it disappeared the further I went, down, and into the dark.

I didn't particularly like the fact that I was leaving a trail that anyone could follow, but follow to what? Nothing. That was the point.

That was why I parked my car four miles away on the other side of the hill in a relatively new neighborhood called Sherman Oaks. The San Fernando Valley was a sleepy area full of orange groves. Peaceful. The perfect place to hide a car.

Peaceful on one side of the hill, and blackness on the other.

It was a simple walk up the hill on the Valley side, then over Mulholland Drive that snaked across the top edge of the hill, then down into the scrub and... everything that waited below.

The lights of Beverly Hills, and Los Angeles beyond, winked from out of the blackness that spread across the land below me.

If I stood a bit, if I stopped and looked down and out to the pool of little lights in the distance that was downtown Los Angeles, I could probably pinpoint right near the location of the Viceroy Hotel that Holly had made her working home in.

I wonder if she hated the men as much as I did, all the ones in the pics.

Maybe she had forgiven them, maybe she had forgotten them the moment after each of them had hurt her.

But maybe she hadn't. Maybe she was resigned to her place in the great mess of the thing, her on the bed, tied tight and paid for her trouble.

I thought of the stash of money she had in the small yellow shoe box, the one never found by anyone but me. I wondered what dreams she had of using it, where she would go.

Maybe she would have gone back home. Maybe she wouldn't have. I like to think that maybe she would have gone back to Montana and picked up her mother. Maybe taken her away, or at least tried to convince her to leave. Convince her that she really didn't have any ropes tying her there. Maybe that's why Holly put up with the ropes here, for the money. I mean that's what it was, but… I also guessed that once you got used to a thing, it was hard to break the habit. Even if it meant you got hurt. A lot.

I wondered why we did that to ourselves. Why I did that to myself.

I liked to think she would have gone home for her mother. If she was still alive.

Mine wasn't. She died three days after I left the farm, but I didn't hear about it for a while until I was in France. And long gone.

She'd fallen out of the hay loft.

The one she'd never been up in a day in her life.

The four mile hike over the hill was nothing. I was used to hikes all throughout my life. From the long ones the Marines took us on in France to kill Germans, to the fast ones I took when I was a kid — running to escape the old man.

I never did do anything about my old man, I couldn't. He

died three years after he killed my mother, and yes — he did kill my mother.

But something about the men I saw in Holly's pics made me want to do something. It wasn't hate. Hate had nothing to do with it anymore.

It was about stopping things.

Besides, I wasn't sixteen anymore.

I used Carlo's ledger, the one I found in the basement of the Hill house. The one with all the records of who and when had been down in that basement for his little black-and-blue parties. I used the names in the ledger and found all seven men — other than the tall bald guy — who were in Holly's pics. All the other names in the ledger, I couldn't be sure that they had done any hitting — any hurting.

My guess is they did hit women, but I couldn't be sure. So I left them alone.

The seven I did find from Holly's pics, let's just say I dropped by each one of them, and convinced them to never do a thing like that again. To any woman.

I wasn't sure if it would do any good, but I had to try. Besides, I'd check in on them from time to time. Make *sure* they didn't do it.

That had been over the course of a week.

Now it was tonight.

And now I stood on the other side of a stone wall that was meant to separate the owner of the house on the other side from any harm.

So I climbed over the wall.

On the other side, was a completely immaculate yard complete with decorative trees and bushes. A peaceful waterfall streamed down from a rock wall constructed exactly for the peace that that water created. A voice of water, telling the owner that everything would always, be all right.

I found out the owner had been married once. The divorce came through after the wife ended up in the hospital for the third time.

194

She got out okay.

But now he was seeing someone else. Looking for another one… to control.

I took a hammer out of my pocket and walked into the house. It was black inside, but I found my way.

I found the tall bald guy in his bed, sleeping. He didn't sleep for long.

I didn't tie him to the bed posts and I didn't gag him, I just hit the tall bald son of a bitch in his own bed until he knifed the air with high-pitched screams like the screaming little pig that he was.

I was glad he had the house up at the end of a very nice road that led up from the flats of Beverly Hills to the end of a small canyon at the base of a hill. Because no one was up there with us. Me and the tall bald guy.

Who got himself hurt.

As in past tense.

Because that's all you have when you're dead.

# Enjoy Devin?

Then grab another — check out the other books and stories in the series:

John Devin, PI — The Novels
   Red is for Blood (Book 1)
   Black is for Hate (Book 2)
   Gold is for Greed (Book 3) — coming soon…

John Devin, PI — Short Stories
   Sunshine (No. 1)
   Bennie (No. 2)

# Could you help out?

A writer's success is based a lot on word of mouth. If you enjoyed this book, please consider leaving an honest review at your favorite retailer, Goodreads, or any other place that great readers gather.

Even a line or two can make all the difference in the world for me, and helps with every writer's greatest wish — to gather a loyal bunch of readers, just like you.

With great appreciation — Michael

# About The Author

Michael Kowal's short fiction appears in multiple volumes of the award winning Fiction River original anthology series. He lives on the central Oregon coast with his wife.

Check in with him online at:

kowalkowal.com.

# Red is for Blood - Sample

Keep reading for the opening Chapters of Book 1 in the John Devin, PI series:

Red is for Blood

And for more about John Devin — and of course all of Michael Kowal's books — visit:

kowalkowal.com

# Red is for Blood - Chapter 1

The fist came at me a split second to midnight, broke my nose at the stroke of, then I heard the band below break into "Jingle Bells." It all smashed together — the fist, my nose, the band, and the pool I was now plummeting toward.

Yeah, the one two stories below me.

It was December 21, 1929.

Merry Christmas to me.

Time slowed like a clock held in mud and that pretty much described my brain at the moment. Fuzzed, slowed, and not thinking too properly. Except I did think of one thing: I hope it's the deep end of the pool.

I hit hard on my back and the water slammed me like concrete. Air shot out of me like a cannon spitting flame, then the cold water rushed in over me.

Numbed, I slowly dropped three, five, and then finally ten feet into the water, until my back softly hit the solid flat surface of the bottom.

Yeah, I'd made it. The

deep end.

It was cold, muffled, and wet down here. Not entirely bad because here nobody was trying to kill me. I opened my eyes, and through the hazy and darkened ten feet of water, saw the edges of the pool above. They were rimmed with Christmas lights and the dark bodies of people who stood in front of them, everyone probably wondering who had decided to take a swim.

Not that they were concerned or anything.

I lay there, on the bottom of the pool, relishing the quiet. It's amazing how still everything is in the water, surrounded by something that doesn't care whether you live or die.

Then a thin, dark, wisping snake of red rose in the water above me. My own blood courtesy of my smashed nose. A thin little reminder from my body that it wanted what was up there. The air that would keep it alive.

Although my brain wasn't sure it wanted to join in that decision.

It was a fight between the two, my brain and my body, the body being the sensible one that wanted to follow the blood topside. My brain, on the other hand, was having its doubts.

It wanted to stay. It was calm down here and what waited above for me was not something it wanted to face. I had gotten into something that I shouldn't, had always sworn I wouldn't, but just this time, just this time only… I did it for the money.

I had to.

Maybe I didn't want to go back up. What it came down to was I had picked a hell of a way to make a living and my brain was lodging a complaint at the moment. Smart one, that brain.

But if I'd listened to it all these years, I would have been dead a hundred times — times twenty. So I went with my gut, as I always did, and pushed my hurt and slammed body off the bottom.

I knew where to go, just follow the trail of my blood back to civilization.

Or what passed for it.

It was late December 1929 and there didn't seem to be a hell of a lot of civilization left these days.

The whole world had started to crack into hell after the crash two months ago. But there was still hope heading into the start of 1930. The hope of the damned, I figured. All of them up there, that's what they celebrated. Me, down here? It seemed the perfect place to close out the '20s. Up there? They all knew what was coming. They just didn't want to admit it. Yet.

But I knew.

So maybe that's why my brain didn't want to head up, but I did anyway.

Back into the city of pain and bright lights.

My home.

Los Angeles.

# Red is for Blood - Chapter 2

I broke the surface to "Jingle Bells," the crowd singing, and a hand ripping me out of the pool by my hair.

Apparently the whole by-the-hair thing didn't matter to anyone, because they just kept drinking, grabbing and grinding each other, everyone well-lubed with the illegal booze that didn't exist.

Welcome to the end of 1929.

The person pulling me up by my hair was Half-a-house. At least that's what I called him. Big as half a house and ugly as a tenement, he had a mustache that tried to make him look like Clark Gable.

It didn't work.

He was the personal bodyguard of one Skyler Gold, the guy I had just been peeking at. Half-a-house grinned at me with a rack of teeth that said I was dead, or at least that I'd soon want to be. "What are you doing here?"

My feet didn't seem to be touching the ground and I was six-feet-and-a-hair as my mother always said. My hair didn't feel too good. "Drip-drying, you mind?"

He slugged me in the gut with his free hand just to get my attention. "I said, what are you doing here. Up there?"

He motioned back to the balcony that he had just thrown me off of. Black wrought iron surrounded it, all curves and thin shapes. It led to two open, white-painted French doors that further led into one of the penthouse suites of the new Hollywood Royal Hotel.

The hotel where apparently all of Los Angeles' best and brightest celebrated Christmas this year.

The central pool was lit and crowded with reds and greens, sparkles, black tuxedoes, jazz, champagne, and highballs. Everything loose and easy, lubed and cocked, flapping away the night like crazed fools running straight into a burning building. Christmas for adults.

I just wanted the hell out of there right now. "I was looking for my wife."

"You don't got no ring."

Half-a-house was observant. "I threw it at her when I kicked her out."

"Then why you lookin' for her?"

I hate logic. Especially from idiots.

"Why don't you let me down and we can talk, civilized, if you know what that is."

Apparently he didn't because instead of letting me drop nice and easy he rammed my head toward the deck and the rest of me followed.

My face plowed straight into the stylish Mexican fiesta-colored tile that surrounded the pool, its second smashing of the night.

I hate this business.

Through the pain and with the energetic energy of the no-fun, twenty-eight-year-old, six-feet, hundred-and-eighty-five-pound ex-Marine that I was — I pile drived my fist straight up into his crotch.

And it slammed into something as hard as a battleship bulkhead.

My knuckles blew out with pain and I just couldn't believe it. He couldn't be that much of a man.

Half-a-house smiled down at me, his bright white teeth just visible under the brim of his light tan fedora.

Then he grabbed my head again, pulled it up knee-high, and as the music dashed into an uphill rag, as the dames and penguins danced off into oblivion, and as I wished like hell I was in some other line of work, Half-a-house's tan-trousered knee ran straight at my face for the final knockout.

And as the knee came up to hit me, a man stepped out from beside Half-a-house and looked straight at me. He wore a white straw hat, a perfect blue suit, and something that didn't really fit into this crowd of swells the color of snow, he was Asian. Not just Asian. Chinese.

I knew Chinese.

And I didn't recognize him.

Then white exploded in my mind and everything went dark. My brain, it seemed, had finally gotten what it wanted.

Peace.

And quiet.

The quiet of the dead.

# Red is for Blood - Chapter 3

I woke wet, cold, and tied at the neck to the red spokes of a smart-looking tan Packard parked along Wilshire. Tied with my own tie. The joke wasn't lost on me.

Cold concrete lay beneath me trying to suck out what little heat I had left in my body. If you listened to the promotions people, Los Angeles was full of all the sun, warmth, and welcome of a church picnic. But what they failed to mention was that it was actually a desert here. Built on a sunbaked hell that at night plunged down into a cold that would almost freeze at certain times of the year. Like this one.

I looked down the sidewalk and there was car after car, all big and expensive, this being the play area of Los Angeles. To the side was the Hollywood Royal I had just been thrown out of, the hotel of choice for the kids of the stars.

Blood dripped from my smashed nose onto my formerly white shirt, my one good one. This night kept getting better and better.

I reached into my jacket, making sure the sleeve didn't get under the dripping blood, and pulled out my switch. The four-inch blade shot out hard and smooth and I got to work on the tie. My only silk tie because I didn't want to look too out of place tonight in the second-fanciest hotel in Los Angeles. Kind of useless, a tie on me. A ribbon on an ox, but there you have it.

The blade made short work of the tie and I was free. A little clock face in light green silk thread was stitched into the fat end of the thing. I threw that end into the gutter and cut up what was left into two small, thin lengths of just the outside silk. Those I pushed up into each side of my bloody and flowing nose.

Use what you got, it's what my old man taught me. So what if it was silk? Celebrate Christmas with a little class.

Half-a-house no more had steel balls than I did.

He must have loaded up with a steel cup. When you babysit

the wild son of the chairman of National Pictures, you know at some point you're bound to take a shot to the cojones.

Yeah, that's Spanish. I pride myself on knowing foreign languages.

The nose would take exactly fifteen minutes for the blood to stop. It's what it always took.

I looked around for my hat out of habit, then remembered I'd lost it somewhere between the first and second stories on the way down to the pool. It had cost me a sawbuck.

I got up off the concrete slow, my whole body aching and especially the ribs. A pain that felt like a fast hot knife stuck in me.

I should never have taken this case but it was done now. I'd seen what I had been hired to see. The bare ass of Skyler Gold, working like an oil derrick into the fresh earth of a blonde chippie that I didn't need to know the name of. Just the fact that there was one and he was working her, instead of one Abigail Thansom.

Miss Thansom. All of twenty and trying to be grown-up and doing a bad job of it. She was in pain but she would be okay, she just needed a few more bottles of wise-up and she would be fine. As bitter and calloused as the rest of us. Well, the rest of them. I passed callous at sixteen.

Killing a man will do that to you.

I headed up Wilshire to the side street where I had left my car. Ahead, searchlights beamed out from the Hollywood Arms Hotel, cutting into the blackened Christmas sky.

The Hollywood Arms was the older brother to the Hollywood Royal. The younger set went to the Royal, and the real power, went to the Arms.

The Arms was a block of concrete, pushed up out of the ground and set at the back of a front yard the size of five football fields. Palms lined the two entrances and ran along the front of the building itself. The place was almost ten years old but still shone bright like the '20s that were crashing around it.

I liked it, on principal. I did like beautiful things, but something about it struck me wrong. The place was filled tonight, as it usually was, with all of Los Angeles' best, drinking the night away at the Papaya Room there.

Politicians, Hollywood types, gangsters, high-up cops, and low-down attorneys, all of them splashing and toasting, rubbing each other all up and down and setting the world right. Their world.

Mine — ours — out here we could all fend for ourselves.

Or so the thinking went.

Out here a guy had to earn a living, which was getting a hell of a lot harder lately. The stock market had crashed two months ago like a wingless airplane, but while everyone said it was just a temporary thing, I wondered if we were in for a long stretch of hurt. Welcome to the 1930s.

It was almost Christmas and the cold of the LA desert cut through me and all I wanted was a wide, short, clear, solid-heavy glass of whiskey in my hand.

And I would get it at O'Hanlon's Deli, which wasn't really a deli.

Doc would be there, too, as he always was. He could patch me up. That is, if he wasn't already laid out.

That was the problem with Doc: he was always drunk, but he was the best I knew at fixing up anything broken or shot.

Luckily it was only the former, but I didn't hold out much hope that sometime soon it wouldn't be the latter.

Or worse.